For Luck's Sake

For Luck's Sake

COZY DUBOIS

Copyright © 2026 by Cozy DuBois

All rights reserved.

No part of this publication may be reproduced, distributed, or transmitted in any form or by any means, including photocopying, recording, or other electronic or mechanical methods, without the prior written permission of the publisher, except as permitted by U.S. copyright law. For permission requests, contact Heartwood Forest Publishing LLC.

The story, all names, characters, and incidents portrayed in this production are fictitious. No identification with actual persons (living or deceased), places, buildings, and products is intended or should be inferred.

Book Cover by Marge Turingan.

Interior Formatting by Cozy DuBois.

Edited by Mikko Lahna.

Paperback ISBN: 978-1-964386-11-9

E-book ISBN: 978-1-964386-10-2

No generative Artificial Intelligence was used in the process of developing, writing, or designing this publication.

First edition 2026

For anyone carrying too much on their shoulders.
Let someone spoil you, even if that means spoiling yourself.

Content Awareness

- Character dealing with grief of past parental loss, including an on-page panic attack.

- Some toxic family and relationship dynamics.

- Explicit sexual content between a trans man and a genderqueer person, with some undernegotiated (but enthusiastically consented to) power dynamics and pain play.

For full details on content warnings (with spoilers), please go to cozydubois.com.

Welcome to Sleighbell Springs!

This festive Christmas town is decked out in tinsel from Thanksgiving to New Year's. But once the last ornament is packed away, and the tour busses roll out, life in this cozy small town carries on.

This multi-author romance series flips the snow globe to show what really happens in Sleighbell Springs the other eleven months a year. From drag queens to booksellers, shop owners of every size to reclusive woodworkers, these stories follow the residents of this small Vermont town as they navigate the quiet seasons, quirky traditions, and unexpected second chances—all while finding love where they least expect it.

Expect cozy vibes, lots of queer joy, found family feels, and a touch of that year-round magic you only find in a town like Sleighbell Springs!

One

Luck

A DOZEN BEAUTIFUL, HALF-NAKED bodies gyrate to the heady music of my dance studio, and I can't help but smile. Junie Hendricks shimmies so skillfully, the silk tassels hanging from her tiddies swing in circles. Aaron Tate practices body rolls in front of the mirror, sweat dripping down his toned abs. A bright purple fan flutters over Estelle du Nord's glorious booty, teasing a peek at her muscular curves.

All of these incredibly hot, sensual beings are thriving in the power of their bodies. Unbound through their newfound self-expression. Freed from the burdens of gender norms and the expectations of respectability that weigh so heavily. And they're having *fun!*

A proud glow warms my chest at the sight of my students laughing, teasing each other, the smirks that hint at their heightened confidence. Here, in the privacy of my dance studio, where I have taught hundreds of students—the sky-high windows draped in thick green curtains to keep out the dark, cold, and any passing eyes—these twelve, brave, *glorious* people are discovering a carefree part of themselves they'd never known.

I should have added burlesque to the class roster years ago.

"Like what you see, Luck?" Estelle teases, brushing the feathers of her fan across my face, before fluttering it over herself again. The bright magenta pops against her brown skin, her hair pulled back into a puff.

"You have never been sexier, babe!" I exclaim, blatantly checking her out, exaggerated so she knows my flirting is platonic.

Estelle giggles anyway, beaming like the sun as she pushes up her glasses. "I've never felt sexier!" She's dressed modestly for burlesque, in a long-sleeve leotard. A far cry from the usual smock she wears while dipping candles and blending oils for perfume, her off-season side hustle here in Sleighbell Springs.

More strikingly is how *differently* she's moving. She's my prima ballerina, our Sugarplum Fairy in the annual run of the Sleighbell Springs *Nutcracker* production. She's normally all elegance—poise and drive protecting the quiet, reserved heart inside. As a Black trans woman in a notoriously traditional form of dance, Estelle has overcome every obstacle through sheer willpower and grace. These fans have brought out a coquettish, playful tease in the regal young woman I've known for years.

"You are beauty, you are grace, you are going to blow everyone's fucking minds with your sexy-ass fan dance at our recital in a few weeks!" I hype her up.

"Oh, don't remind me!" Avery Evans moans from the floor a few feet away, where they're velcroing their faux-leather pants back together after they tore them off during their showcase preview earlier. Avery and a few other trans masc students (the friends who roped the anxious Avery into signing up for this class in the first place) are doing a campy classic rock number. Of the group, Avery is the one most unsure of stripping onstage.

I was hoping that by being in a group, Avery would feel more confident. No one is obligated to show any part of their body that they don't want to, or even perform at the showcase. Especially not someone the same age as my baby brothers, even though Avery, Luis, and Efrain are all twenty-one now. However, Avery keeps stubbornly insisting that they want to, sometimes even in the same breath as they bemoan how much they're dreading their performance.

I am choosing to trust that they're simply voicing their anxiety. They're a lot like my best friend Felix that way: obstinate, but surprisingly agreeable and kind behind those grumpy words. I remind myself that Felix was well into his drag king career by Avery's age, and I had already moved on from the burlesque scene by then—too busy raising my brothers. Maybe grappling with the reality that I'm mere weeks from turning thirty is making me feel ancient, but twenty-one seems so incredibly young.

"None of that now, Avery!" I tease. My role here is to be encouraging, after all, not reminisce about my lost youth. "Remember, why do you want to do this?"

Avery nods, overly serious, blue eyes wide and slightly haunted looking. "Because I want to tear my pants off onstage, Full Monty-style, at least once in my life."

"That's the spirit!" I can never get a read on Avery, but I smile at them anyway. The rest of the class has stopped their practice to listen. I glance at the clock. As it was, I was going to stop them in a few minutes, so I take the opportunity for a pep talk. "Legally, in Vermont, we can't go Full Monty at the Sleighbell Stage, but we can tear our pants off! And shake our asses!" I pop my hips a few times and shake my chest. "And shimmy our bodies in whatever way feels powerful and good and sexy!"

The class grins, shimmying along with me. There's only three weeks before the spring equinox, when Sleighbell Springs' first ever burlesque recital is scheduled, and I have never had so much fun in March!

"You've mastered the basics, your solos are looking phenomenal, and all of you have been working so hard! This recital is going to be so fucking hot, spring will come early to Sleighbell Springs!" I grin as Aaron whoops, doing another body roll, simply because he fucking wants to. I love every single person in this class for their bravery, their vulnerability, their openness to trying something new and shocking for this small town. I was an overeager dance major when I took my first burlesque class, as an extracurricular in my first year of Julliard over a decade ago; I can't imagine taking it for the first time as a busy, responsible adult. "Because we're what?"

"Sexy Santas!" the class shouts the nickname they picked for themselves the first day of class.

I laugh, delighted at their Christmas spirit. As soon as they picked it, I knew Felix would tease me relentlessly. And he has, several times. But unlike his Scroogy ass, most of us love living in a Christmas town. Our whole economy revolves around it; why wouldn't it become a core part of our personalities?

"Damn straight!" I cheer. "And in three short weeks, we're going to put on a performance Sleighbell Springs will never forget!" Bending down, I rap my knuckles on the studio floor. "Knock on wood!"

The class chuckles, their smiles easier after a pep talk. Even the owl-eyed Avery is grinning, nodding along with me. Their friends, Keiran, Aiden and Nome, bring Avery into their own small group handshake. It always seems to get more complicated and confusing each time they do it, but I love seeing younger queer folks with their own inside jokes. Even if I'm getting too old to understand them.

"That's it for our class today, but keep practicing at home, and working on those costumes! Remember, we're having a pasties and sequins meetup on Saturday morning! We want outfits you can move in, that you feel good in, and that you can whip off without getting stuck!" I clap once, my usual signal that class is over. Everyone disperses, gathering up their stripper droppings and accessories. "Get home safe everyone!"

"Luck, you want a ride?" Junie asks, pulling a sweatshirt back over her head, an Ugly Christmas design advertising Sleigh Queen. One of the trans masc crew, Aiden Cane, designs unhinged sweaters for every business in town. The Sleigh Queen sweater features a cartoon version of May North, riding the iconic disco moose. "I think they said it might snow."

My gut clenching, I glance at the windows, where green velvet covers the floor-to-ceiling glass of the showroom. During the day, they're open, filling the former car dealership with bright sunshine, just like when my parents owned it. They're closed now, hiding the snowclouds that have been looming all day, as much as protecting my student's privacy.

Junie's probably right. It's smelled like snow since this morning; I wouldn't be surprised if it already started. This might be a proper storm. March weather can be so fickle.

With a heavy swallow, I force a smile. "Oh, no! You know I love biking!"

"Yeah, everyone in Sleighbell Springs knows you love biking, Luck," Junie teases, wrapping her scarf around her. Her plump figure is soon buried in her parka. "Thought I'd ask, anyway. Get home safe, okay? It's dark already."

"A little dark and snow can't stop me!" I wink. "Besides, I'm right down the street."

I clean up as everyone files out to their cars, calling their goodbyes in the parking lot. I've loved Dancers and Prancers ever since I was a kid, when I'd hang out here with Jorge and "help" our parents restore and sell collectible cars. I miss those days, though I'm glad we managed to keep the showroom in the family, even if the cars are long gone. A combination dance studio and mechanic may not be the legacy my parents dreamed of, but they'd be proud that their older kids can live our passions, and afford to send the younger two to college to find theirs.

Before Luis and Efrain went back to school in January, I spontaneously opened enrollment for a burlesque class, to keep the off-season sadness from catching a hold of me. Usually, I'm left listless when the holiday season is over. This year? I couldn't let that happen. My lovely, adventurous students trusted me to guide them safely into their sensual sides, to get us through the post-holiday winter blues together.

I love ballet, I love tap, I love teaching, and producing the annual run of *The Nutcracker* ballet is my favorite time of year. But once the lights go off after New Year's, so does my passion for it. For everything, really. However, this year, I'm determined to get ahead of the seasonal depression and sad slog of early spring. I'm turning thirty and reclaiming my life, one day at a time, finding purpose beyond ballet and my brothers.

With one last check to make sure Jorge locked up the service garage before he left, I strap my saddlebag to Bertha, my trusty fat tire bike, and clip my helmet under my chin. "Ready, bella?"

Flurries swirl in the dark sky as I push Bertha through the side door. The cold wind cuts through my coat and makes my eyes water. The door slams open wider than it's supposed to, knocking over the bucket of road salt my brother stashed next to the door.

Righting the bucket and pushing the cover closed again, I curse under my breath. I have no idea if spilling road salt is bad luck. But I can't afford anything but good fortune the next few weeks, at least until after the recital.

"Probably best to apply the same rules as table salt. Right?" With my mittened hands, I scoop up as much salt as I can and toss it over my shoulder onto the sidewalk. The snowstorm brings me enough anxiety alone; opening up myself to bad luck like that only makes me dread what's to come. "Everything will be okay. I did what I could. That's what matters!" I breathe through the pang in my chest and push off down the road towards home. "At least it hasn't started accumulating yet!"

My brother and I live less than a mile down the street, and yet everyone in Sleighbell Springs thinks I'm nuts for biking all winter long. But there's power in each pump of my legs, my hands gripping the handlebars through my mittens. The whir of Bertha's tires under the slushy pavement connects me to the ground. The rush of air stinging my eyes makes me one with the wind. The snowflakes on my skin are tiny kisses from Mother Nature.

On a bike, I am free. I am safe. I am powerful.

AT HOME, I DON'T go inside. My heart heavy, I rack Bertha beside her sister, Leann (my road bike for the warmer months), on the stand inside the garage. The snow is falling steadily now, gusts of wind blowing in through the garage door. Jorge will probably get annoyed at me for letting the snow in; he's so meticulous about keeping the heated three-car garage tidy. But he hasn't cleaned the kitchen in weeks, so I can't bring myself to care.

I tug my gear off piece by piece, hanging it on the rack to dry for tomorrow. Luckily, other teachers are in charge of the morning classes. I just have a meeting at the community theater around lunchtime, and a few after-school youth classes. My mittens and scarf should dry before I need to go anywhere.

Pulling back the tarp in the corner of the garage, I drag my hand across the hood of the seafoam green '57 Eldorado, a silent greeting to childhood memories of holding the flashlight for my dad while he worked on it. He was restoring Dancer for me, he said, and he'd finish it as soon as I was mature and sensible enough to appreciate it. I would tease him back, saying he'd never finish it in that case, because I was too much of a free spirit to be sensible or mature.

He never did have the chance. My free spirit was forced to learn too quickly how to be sensible and mature, for the sake of my younger brothers.

I pop open the passenger door, and slide into the bench seat, breathing in the scent of old leather, dust, and the faded "new car" air freshener. Through the dusty windshield, snow falls in thick flakes. I touch the bright green rabbit's foot my dad hung from the rearview mirror, along with the silver charm of St. Christopher. "Hello, Dancer."

A few years ago, Jorge finished restoring his own project car that Dad meant to give him, a cherry red '68 Firebird that Dad named Dasher. Then Jorge fixed up our younger brothers' cars (Comet and Cupid, a blue '67 Corvette and an orange '69 Camaro, respectively). Both are still in storage at Dancers and Prancers, waiting to be their college graduation presents next year.

As if sensing I didn't want him to, Jorge never offered to work on the Eldorado. It's been nine years, two months, and thirt—no!—*almost two weeks* since the accident, and I still can't bear the idea of working on it without Dad. Just like how Jorge gets quiet and surly when I suggest putting away Mom's elaborate and eclectic collection of holiday decorations. The coqui and maga flower ornaments on the Christmas tree stay up year round. The festive wreath on our front door is worn and faded. The "Feliz Navidad" sign hanging from it is barely legible after a decade, but I've never pushed. We both have parts of them we can't let go of.

My eyes are burning, the snow a blur, when a light splits through the dark. The mudroom door shuts quietly, and the driver's side door opens.

A ball of curly red fur and wet-dog smell hits me. Olive, Jorge's emotional support dog, greets me with kisses, stepping all over me in her excitement. Like her unconventional coat for a Golden Retriever, Olive isn't the calmest emotional support dog. She failed out of her service dog program she'd been bred and raised for, which is how we got so lucky as to be able to afford her for Jorge with the last of the estate money. Jorge is too calm, too quiet, too withdrawn; she's a good balance for him.

My brother slides into the driver's seat on Olive's other side, his hoodie pulled up over his head. Only a few black waves poke out over his eyes. "You good?"

"Yeah," I smile. He's so predictable. Much like Felix, Jorge acts tough, invulnerable. Inside, he's a big softy. My brother hides his feelings well, but the signs are there. Sometimes, he even talks about them. "You?"

"Course," he mutters. "Olive was wondering where you were."

"Oh, was she?" I scratch Olive's ears, leaning away from her cold nose when she snuffles my face.

"I figured you were out here being a mopey bitch, like usual." He shrugs. "But she wanted to make sure. Got her big puppy dog eyes by the door, you know, laid on the guilt thick. Had to get up and check to make sure my sister—sorry, hermane—was still alive."

"Sister is fine, you know. I might be genderqueer, but I'm still the eldest daughter in this family." I snort, grateful he's not making a fuss about me crying in Dad's car.

"Nah, hermane fits you." Jorge clears his throat. "Wanna talk about it?

I shake my head. "Just...missing them, I guess."

He leans back in his seat, crossing his arms. "It'll be spring soon. We won't have as many storms like this."

I nod, unsure if I want fewer reminders. This time of year is always the hardest, but I cherish all of the memories that come with the heavy snowfalls, just like the night of the accident. The rest of the year, the memories are less frequent, but they don't fill me with guilt. In a snowstorm? The grief is bitter, laced with anger at myself, at them, at all of the circumstances that led to their loss. It's there, and it's raw, and I feel them so much closer when it hurts.

"We're going to get a damn snowdrift in here if we don't go in soon." Jorge opens his door, nodding at me to do the same. "Come on, I'll make you some hot cocoa or something. Sitting alone in the garage like this is just pitiful."

A mischievous grin breaks across my face. Already halfway out the door, I giggle in my rush to get out of the way, in case Olive follows me instead of Jorge when I say the magic word, "With *cheese*?"

Like an activated sleeper agent, Olive leaps frantically, shoving Jorge out of the way in her excitement for the cheese tax. She leaps at the door to the mudroom, pawing at the handle until she's let herself in. It's service dog skill that someone with her temperament should never have learned, because she only uses it for selfish reasons. Like stealing cheese, escaping from bath time, or breaking into my room before I'm awake to throw her empty food bowl at my head, even though *Jorge* is the one who feeds her.

"You had to get her riled up, didn't you?" Jorge shakes his head in disgust, but there's a smile on my brother's face and a twinkle in his brown eyes. "Of course, with cheese. What kind of Boricuas would we be if we don't have cheese in our hot cocoa?"

"The kind who were born and raised in Vermont, probably." I grab my saddlebag from Bertha, and follow him inside. "But Mom would be happy we still put cheese in our hot cocoa, so of course we will." I raise an eyebrow at him. "Are you gonna do the dishes too, for once?"

"I always do my dishes. Yours are just always in the way!" Jorge scoffs when he shuts the garage door. A surge of love for my brother makes me smile. As the eldest, I have been taking care of him since Efrain and Luis came along, when we were eight and five. The twin terrors kept our parents busy, and it fell on me to step in for the newly minted middle child.

With the boys now in college out of state, and the ten year anniversary of our parents' death this coming December, Jorge now keeps me grounded—a living reminder of the love our parents had for all four of us. Between him and Felix, I'm surrounded by grumps who take care of me, just as much as I take care of them.

Two

Luck

Close to noon, Burl Cane waves at me as his snowplow rumbles past my house, clearing the bike lane for me. The fresh fallen snow covering my street is cheery and bright, the late season drifts so pristine and sparkling that I can't help but smile. This tight-knit town looks after everyone. Even the weirdos like me, who cycle all winter long, despite being nestled in a valley of the Green mountains.

The snowstorm last night dumped eight inches on Sleighbell Springs, but it couldn't have been *that* bad if Burl is already doubling back to clear the bike lanes. Not as bad as last month's monster blizzard, anyway! Sure enough, Burl's son Aiden (my burlesque student who makes the ugly sweaters, like the Candy Cane Cafe one I'm wearing today) follows after him a few moments later in the sweeper, cleaning up the sidewalks. After a bad storm, I'm usually stuck walking to Dancers and Prancers for a few days.

"Ready to go, Bertha?" I buckle my helmet under my chin, tugging my scarf up. I tap her thick tires with my toe, checking that she's got enough pressure for the ride into town. I don't want to be late for my lunch meeting with Twyla and Nisha!

With a smile as bright as the sunshine and blue skies above, I set off for the town square, where we're planning the lighting and set design for our recital at the Sleighbell Stage Community Theater in a few weeks.

The ride to the square is quick, but scenic, with the majestic mountains and acres of forest surrounding our little town in the valley. Snow and ice crunches under my tires, but trusty Bertha doesn't slip. The cheerful year-round holiday decor looks festive covered in the clean, fresh powder. After the busy season ended with New Year's, most of the holiday cheer went away. I packed away the *Nutcracker* costumes and sets, and in town, all of the temporary decor—the tinsel, inflatables, and roadside shops—has been carefully stored away for next year. But Christmas never really dies in this place. Even in March, the Easter bunnies wear Santa hats, and our leprechauns are merely North Pole elves adorned with top hats and clovers.

The town square is as delightful as always, an eclectic mix of charming facades leading me down Mistletoe Street. In front of the church, I spot Felix hauling a ladder behind his dad and brother, but my destination is the three-story brick building a few blocks from the square. I can say hi later. A glittering marquee, supported by pillars with candy cane striping and adorned with evergreen bunting, reads "Sleighbell Stage" in green letters. It's the only venue in town with a large enough stage for the giant cast of ballerinas and dancers for our annual *Nutcracker* performances. So, of course, it's where I need my first burlesque show to be too!

I lock Bertha up securely on the bike rack outside, and tug my saddlebag off. Not that I don't trust folks in Sleighbell Springs, but I don't want her to fall and bend a spoke. Jorge might be the mechanic in the family, but I am also our father's child; keeping my bikes in good shape is second nature for me, too. After that ride, her frame is splattered in slush and salt. "We'll get you all cleaned up when we get home, okay, bella?"

When I walk in, Twyla and Nisha McKay are nowhere to be seen. The grand entrance of the theater is strangely quiet, even for a weekday in the off-season. The lights are off, leaving the grand red velvet tapestries drab. The extensive woodwork of the staircases into the theater, normally shiny with polish, seem dull in the low light.

Did they forget our meeting? I smile through the pang in my chest. While it's unlike the owners of the Sleighbell Stage to forget anything, I would understand. This meeting probably isn't a high priority for them. It's not like this recital is the only thing fueling me through the worst part of the year, or anything. It's just a one-night show that they're doing as a favor to me; we have time to reschedule a quick lunch meeting.

However, as my very close friends, Twyla and Nisha should remember that this class is important to *me*. It's the only source of light I've had since the busy season ended, to help me cope with off-season sadness and the grief I'm attempting to unpack. To combat my growing burnout with the endless classes that always get set aside for the same fucking show year after year after year—

I sigh, trying to calm my racing heart. "No, this isn't about me." This is about Aaron and Junie, Estelle and Avery, and helping everyone blossom into the newfound confidence that I've seen emerge over the past six weeks. I can't let them down.

I stalk up the stairs, hoping Nisha and Twyla are somewhere within, even though they both usually prefer to work from the box office.

The theater is colder than I expected. As I shiver, a sigh of relief escapes me when I see Twyla and Nisha McKay in a tender embrace near the stage, in the center of a wide spotlight. I can't help but smile at the intimacy between these two lovely Black women, my dear friends who I first met in New York.

I clear my throat, my breath misting. "Sorry to interrupt the moment— You're crying!" Nisha's round cheeks are wet, and even the stoic Twyla is looking away from me, her jaw tight. "What's wrong? What happened? Who are we fighting?"

Nisha wipes her eyes as she pulls her face out of the crook of her wife's neck. "Oh, Luck! I'm so sorry, I forgot about our meeting!" She sniffles, wiping her face. "I should have called you this morning to tell you."

"Tell me what?" I ask.

Twyla gestures around her, as if the answer should be obvious.

I blink, wondering what she's talking about when it hits me. They're not standing in a spotlight; they're standing in *sunlight*. A circle of plaster and brick and snow surrounds them, covering the vintage jacquard seats and worn carpet running along the center aisle.

"Oh no," I whisper, looking up. "The salt did this." The sun looks back at me through the ceiling, as if taunting us with his cheerful innocence. My stomach sinks. "Oh, no, no no, this cannot be happening. One handful wasn't enough!"

"Trust me, I've pinched myself several times since we got here this morning," Twyla sighs, shaking her head. The beads in her box braids click together. "The last thing we need is another setback like this."

"How long will it take to fix?" I ask, hating that I'm already making this about me, but I feel responsible for Twyla and Nisha, too. When the previous owners retired, I invited them here to become the theater's new owners. They'd been talking about escaping the city for a quieter life since I met them over a decade ago. I almost cried from relief when the sale went through two years ago; if they hadn't stepped in and bought it, the future of the Sleighbell Stage would have been short.

So of course, their time as the new owners has been one disaster after another: the sound system needed replacing right away, the basement flooded when a water main broke last spring, there was an old lien on the building the previous owners forgot about, so they couldn't do repairs for months, and so on.

"I don't know that we can, Luck." Nisha's face crumples again, and Twyla pulls her tighter, brushing her tears away with a gentle caress of her cheek. "Our insurance is already sky-high from all the repairs we've done, and this is going to need a structural engineer, and—"

"One step at a time, babe," Twyla reminds her, kissing her wife's forehead. "We call the insurance, and I dunno, go buy a tarp or something? Maybe we can sell it as-is, cut our losses—"

"Felix!" I shout, unwilling to let Twyla finish that sentence.

"What?" Twyla looks at me like I've grown a second head.

"Felix can help! He's a structural engineer, kind of. Well, he's got the degree! And he can fix it! Felix can fix anything! He renovated my bathroom!" I ramble, the words tumbling out of me the longer Twyla and Nisha stare at me blankly. "He even put in a tankless water heater. And he turned the showroom into a dance studio. And all sorts of stuff!"

Twyla frowns, shaking her head. "Ho Ho Handyman did some work for us after last month's storm, and somehow ended up owing *us* money. Which he still hasn't paid back. I don't trust Joe not to land us further in debt, when we already can't afford this."

"Not Ho Ho Handyman!" I wave my hands, as if that might shoo their hesitation away. "Hire Felix, not his dad. Felix will get it done! Fast and cheap!" Desperation leaks into my voice. I probably shouldn't make promises like this for Felix, but I can talk him into it. "He'll even do it at cost!"

"Even if he did it at cost, I doubt we can even afford that," Nisha sighs, rubbing her neck. "I'm sorry, Luck. I had such high hopes for this place, but we've had so many unexpected costs since we took it over. And with this being a historic building, and significant structural damage, it'll probably be months before a claim goes through. Unless the insurance company can pull some miracle and get us the money faster than they did last time, we're going to have to close."

"No!" I shake my head, stubbornness bubbling like nausea in my belly. "Let me talk to Felix, we'll patch this for now! Enough to keep you open until the insurance comes through!"

"Patch it with what, Luck? Supplies cost money, even if you convince Felix to work for free. And we don't have ceiling collapsing money." Twyla runs a hand over her face. "It's March! We're not going to make a profit on any show in Sleighbell Springs until at least November."

"The burlesque show!" I blurt out, pacing back and forth outside the circle of plaster and melting snow that coats the red carpet and gold upholstered seats. Twyla and Nisha may be hopeless right now, but delusion is my greatest strength. My mind is already flowing with ideas, so fast that I can't talk quickly enough to keep up. "We can make it a benefit show! With the drag queens from Sleigh Queen, and aerialists, and pole dancers from Jingle My Bells! You'll see!" I gesticulate wildly as I talk, needing them to understand even a fraction of my vision. "This town loves a holiday theme, and it's Easter, it's St. Patrick's, the spring equinox! We'll call it..." I pause, letting the ideas coalesce. "Sleighbell Spring Awakening! Tying in the sex and power themes of the play—not the musical, so we don't have to pay any licensing fees! It'll be a sexy, sensual spectacle the likes of which Sleighbell Springs has never seen before!"

Twyla and Nisha exchange a look, deferring to each other with a subtle nod, and I know I've won. There's hope in their eyes.

"We'll draw the whole town here, if it means keeping this place open!" I beam, my trusty optimism warm in my chest. "Sleighbell Springs doesn't leave anyone out in the cold! This town will come together for you!" I gasp. "Ooh, a silent auction? Yes! Great idea!"

As long as I can get Felix on board, anyway. We have to fix this hole first— I gasp, another idea springing to life. "This is perfect!" I whisper.

If I'm already asking the drag *queens*, maybe I can bring back my favorite dance partner, my co-captain from our championship-winning high school dance team, currently employed by Sleigh Queen as a go-go dancer and drag king.

People are always asking me and Felix if we're ever going to get together; if Sleighbell Springs wants to see us dance like we did back in our glory days, so much that they're still asking about it over a decade later, they'll for sure turn up to see us in a number together! Now that we're both our authentic selves, instead of closeted trans teens performing hyperfemininity, any dance we do together is going to set this whole town on fire with how hot it is!

"Oh, Felix is going to hate this."

"Hate what?" Nisha asks.

"But Sleighbell Springs? They're going to love it!" I grin, bouncing on my feet. "And so will I!"

"Love what?" Twyla asks. "Babe, do you have any idea what they're talking about?"

"This is the best idea ever!" I throw my arms around them both, before skipping out of the theater.

I have a Scroogy best friend to track down.

Three

Felix

THE FIRST SIGN THAT my day is about to go very wrong is my little brother smirking down at me from the top of the ladder, where he is *supposed* to be reattaching the metal cable to the streetlight, so we can get the string lights across the square back up.

Rudy pulls down his balaclava as he shoots me a grin, just to make sure I can see he's about to say something out of pocket.

"What?" I huff. "You better not be creeping in anyone's window again."

"Fuck off, that was one time!" Rudy rolls his eyes, turning back to ratchet the bolt that will tighten down the cable. "And Junie wasn't exactly complaining. She DMed me a nude after."

"You're such a creep."

"Better than a coward."

I grumble under my breath, tempted to kick the ladder I'm spotting.

"Look alive, boys!" As if sensing our impending fight, our dad waits one streetlight down at the other end of the cable, ready to pull it taut at Rudy's signal. At least the extensive lighting suspension cables strung around the square had the grace to fall during the off-season. Unlike the last ice storm in November that took out the lights down Mistletoe Street, we don't have Sleighbell Springs utility department breathing down our necks to get the infrastructure back up before nightfall. "Felix, pay attention!"

"Why me?" I call back, bristling in defensiveness. "Rudy's the one talking shit!"

"I don't care about your bickering!" Dad points behind me. "You have a visitor. Don't get distracted! Safety first!"

My heart leaps into my throat as I whirl around, already knowing who it is. Rudy is gonna be such an annoying little shit the rest of the day, but I can't bring myself to care.

As predicted, Luck is making a beeline toward me, pushing their winter bike alongside them; the fat tires crunch over the fresh layer of snow. When they see me looking back at them, a smile blooms across their face and they hop a little as they wave, practically skipping in excitement.

The butterflies in my stomach do the same, a flurry of excitement that Luck is seeking me out. It's a portent of bad news, but my veins practically hum from joy anyway.

"Hi Mr. Joe Kelly!" Luck waves to my dad, calling him by the nickname they've called him since we met at the Little Tykes Tap class in kindergarten. "Some storm we had, huh? Lot of damage to repair?"

"This storm will keep us busy for a while, Miss Lucia!" My dad returns, beaming a fond smile. "But we'll manage. Ho Ho Handyman always does!"

Everyone in our family—hell, everyone in Sleighbell Springs—is soft on Luck, none more so than me. Dad has offered to change his greeting to Mx. Luck, but they insist they like it when he calls them Miss Lucia, purely for the nostalgia. The feminine version of their name doesn't bother them the way my deadname does; Luck simply suits them better.

"Rudy, how was your date last week?" Luck asks my brother, calling up the ladder. Their superstitious ass keeps their distance from it, like they do every ladder, so they don't accidentally walk under it somehow. "You took Ara to Velveteen Crumbs, right?"

I wrinkle my nose; what business does my brother have dating my drag mother's niece?

Rudy simply laughs. "Can't keep anything private around here."

"You gonna see her again?" Luck teases, just as nosy as everyone else in this damn town.

"Probably not." Rudy grins down the ladder. "Sorry to disappoint, but ya boy's still on the market!"

"She turned you down, didn't she?" I ask. "Smart girl."

"I know *you're* not talking shit about *my* love life!" Rudy warns, waving his wrench over his shoulder at me.

"So...Felix!" Thankfully, Luck changes the subject. They turn their doe eyes to me, a hesitant smile playing at their lips that I know can only mean trouble. "My oldest, dearest friend."

"What do you want?" I huff; Luck is so ham-fisted when it comes to manipulation. But Luck doesn't need to be good at it to get what they want. They're charming enough that they only have to ask anyone for anything, and everyone in town will give them the clothes off their back.

Luck's smile flickers into a wince. "Did you hear about the community theater?"

I shake my head. "We've been working on restringing the light cables all morning."

Even Luck's wince fades. There's a slight hitch to their breath before they answer that sends my heart to my stomach. "The roof collapsed in the storm last night."

"Shit, are Twyla and Nisha okay?" I blurt out, hand tightening around the ladder. Aside from me, they're Luck's closest friends. "Was anyone hurt?"

"Oh, no! They're fine!" Luck waves a hand, attempting to put a smile back on their face. "Physically anyway. Emotionally, not so much. Financially? Things are dicey. They might—" Luck looks around, lowering their voice. "They might have to close. For good."

"What?" I whisper. "Why?"

"Something with the insurance that I didn't really pry into, but Nisha was crying, and Twyla was so anxious. I feel awful," Luck murmurs, squeezing their eyes shut. "I need your help."

"Anything." It escapes my lips before I can second-guess it. Normally, I'd give them a hard time, tease them a bit. But after three decades of friendship, Luck's face is an open book. That crinkle in their chin, the lines between their brows, the subtle bite to their full lips—Luck is genuinely upset.

"Can you help patch the roof, a short-term fix to keep them open?" They ask, pausing to bite their lip again, but not long enough for me to answer. "I want to turn the burlesque recital into a fundraiser and help raise the money for them to stay open long enough to fight the insurance company to pay the claim. But to do that, we need the auditorium, and it's a historic building, so we need someone who knows what they're doing, and you're so good at roofing and carpentry, and you have a structural engineering degree, and I trust you to—"

"When do you need it by?" I interrupt their rambling, already feeling torn. If the roof collapsed, I'm not sure how "patching" it will help. But I can at least take a look. While Dad needs all the free labor he can get right now, he'll understand if I help out with this. He'd do the same thing, if he wasn't behind schedule on jobs he's already spent the advances on.

Luck winces again. "Our show is in three weeks. I want to raise enough for the parts and labor for you, and help give the theater a little cushion to cover everything, but they can't afford to pay anything up front."

I huff. Ho Ho Handyman doesn't have the credit to cover the cost for materials, or to spare me for that long.

But for Luck?

I'll figure it out. We'll manage, like Dad always says.

"Hey Dad!" Rudy calls. "Can you fire Felix for about three weeks?"

"Fire me?" I grumble. "We're basically volunteers." Dad is about six months behind on our paychecks, but Rudy lives at home, and I make enough in tips at Sleigh Queen every weekend to pay my bills. Rudy and I both do our part to keep his business from going under, and hope that if and when he comes into a good job, he'll remember how much he owes us.

"Yeah, of course! We'll manage! He's all yours, Luck!" Dad calls. "You done tightening that yet, Rude?"

"Give 'er a tug!" Rudy yells back.

"Really?" I huff, secretly relieved I don't have to ask Dad; all four of us know I'm all in on whatever Luck asks of me. "Don't I get a say in this?"

"Oh, thank you!" Luck throws their arms around my neck, bumping the ladder.

"Hey, watch it!" Rudy calls, bracing himself with the cable he just secured.

"Sorry!" Luck calls.

I can't respond. The molasses scent of their hair fills my senses, and the strength in their arms squeezes me tight. I fight to keep from gathering Luck in my arms and never letting go. Once I get a grip on myself, I pat their shoulder. "Yeah, whatever."

They step away, the mischievous smile back on their expressive face. "There's one more thing."

I shake my head, eager to tease them again. "No."

"Felix!" they whine. "Come on, you don't even know what it is yet!"

"I don't need to!" I retort. They're so cute when they scrunch their nose like that. "You got that look on your face that tells me you're nothing but bad news."

They gasp, offended. "I'm the best news! I promise you, it's going to be so much fun!"

"Nope!"

"Felix, at least let me say what it is!" Luck pleads.

I roll my eyes, loving how they brighten, because they know I'm giving in. "Fine. What is it."

"So my burlesque class is turning into a fundraiser, right?"

"Yeah?" I don't like this already. Luck knows I don't do dance classes anymore.

"Well, our recital is maybe thirty minutes, max. And that's not going to raise the money we need!" Luck gets that light in their eyes, whenever they get a big idea. "So we need to think bigger! I'm thinking silent auction, bougie concessions, raffles! More acts, more star power, more sexy! So, I'm going to invite other sexy performers in town to join us!" They clap, cheesing at me expectantly.

I raise an eyebrow. No one stresses themself out as much as Luck Alvarez. But when they get an idea, they can't let it go. Like Olive and her tennis ball obsession: she loves to fetch them, but not give them back so we can throw them again. Luck gets huge ideas, works themself to exhaustion making them happen, then gets depressed when it's over. And I'm there to support them through every single one. "What does that have to do with me?"

"Because you, Mr. Drag King, will be one of those sexy performers, who brings all of that star power and more!" Luck gushes, clutching my bicep. "Everyone in town loves you, and they would pay good money to see us back together on the stage!"

My stomach drops. Of course. "Luck, we haven't danced together since—"

"Exactly, Felix!" Luck bounces in excitement. "We won state as co-captains for the dance team back in the day! Imagine, one night only, the two of us together onstage again, only all grown up and smoking hot!" Their eyes catch mine, and my heart thumps in my chest. "Everyone in town thinks we peaked in high school, Felix. Let's show them we're still superstars!"

"We did peak in high school," I wince. "Or at least, *I* did. You went to Julliard, and I'm an underpaid handyman."

"No, you are Santa's head elf!" Luck taps my nose. "And the sexiest drag king in town!"

"That doesn't mean everyone else wants to see—"

"Two numbers, that's all I ask, Felix," Luck breathes, stepping closer to me to squeeze my arm. "One intro to open the show, and a double act with me before intermission." Their hand drags from my bicep to my chest, and their touch burns even through my insulated coat. If they only had any sense of what they were doing to me right now... "You thrive onstage, Felix. You're charming, and charismatic, and funny. The Sleighbell Stage needs performers like that. Twyla and Nisha need you." They bite their lip in a way that is too natural to be an act. They're so blatant about their coercion, I can't even be mad that they're taking advantage of my feelings like this. "I need you."

My breath catches as they look up at me through their eyelashes, brown eyes wicked in their smirk. My attempt to grumble comes out more like a whimper.

"Think about it, Felix," Luck murmurs, so close the scent of molasses consumes me. "The roof is help enough, of course, but if you want to help save our friend's theater, stop by Dancers and Prancers tonight at eight. Let's see how well we dance together, after all this time." They wink. "I'll make sure Jorge works late too. You should stop in and harass him for a bit."

My mouth is dry when I manage to whisper, "I'll think about it."

"That's all I ask, Felix," Luck kisses my cheek, and the soft press of their lips against my chilled skin makes my face burn. I'm probably as red as my hair right now. Ham-fisted or not, I am wrapped around their little finger—have been since we were kids—and there's nowhere else I'd rather be. "See you tonight."

They're halfway down the block, riding Bertha towards their dance studio, by the time I remember how to breathe again. It takes Rudy stomping down the ladder and punching me in the arm to come back to my senses.

"See you tonight, Felix," he teases, mimicking Luck's soft voice. He bends over to pick up the toolbox, laughing at me as he wiggles his hips. "I need you, Felix. Shake your ass for the whole town, Felix."

"Shut the fuck up, dickhead!" I aim a kick at him, and my pesky little brother jumps out of the way, laughing. "I'm just thinking about it!"

"Nah, we all know you're gonna do it!" Rudy rolls his eyes. "Luck didn't need to lay it on that thick. You're their little bitch!"

I huff, collapsing the ladder down to bring it to the next light pole. Rudy's an annoying little shit, but he's not wrong. Everyone in town knows how I feel about them, even if Luck doesn't want to acknowledge it out loud. I might have a reputation for being a Scrooge, but as far as Luck is concerned, I'm a pushover.

Still, my chest is tight with guilt; I might have to say no to Luck for once. While dance is my freedom now, being part of a recital like this... that might be more than I can give.

"This is bullshit, man!" I scuff my toe against a crack in the concrete. Waiting for Luck's last class to end, I'm killing time on the mechanics side of Dasher's and Prancer's with Jorge. Mostly by venting to their brother about the impossible position Luck's put me in.

Olive thinks I'm pointing at something. She snuffles the ground near my foot, looking for food, even though her mouth is full of a tennis ball she wants me to throw but is unwilling to hand over. Her tail wags, slapping the back of my knees through my quilted coveralls.

Despite the chill air in the spacious garage, I'm sweating in my winter gear. However, I don't plan to stick around long enough to take it off. I'm just going to tell Luck that I'll do the repairs, but I'm not comfortable with being in their show, and leave.

Whether I do this recital or not, our friendship is going to suffer. Might as well go the route that won't blow it up completely.

Jorge merely grunts in response, elbow deep in repairing the transmission of a hearse. Jorge is as much of a pushover as Luck; he only charges tourists full price. Many of the businesses in town, including the Forever Holiday Funeral Home, bring their repairs to him.

"Not the job itself, because Luck was being a bit dramatic by saying the roof collapsed. The hole isn't that big. But you know my dad's shit with money!" I grumble, squatting down to scratch Olive's ears. She pants around the tennis ball, offering me her butt instead. I pet the curly red fur of her back and hips, snorting at her funny stomps as I scritch all of her good spots. "And I'm supposed to find the materials for this repair on credit? What credit? The hardware store said we can't buy more material until our current invoices are all paid up!"

As expected, Jorge doesn't respond.

"I'll manage, of course. Because I want to help Twyla and Nisha, too!" I frown. "And like, the theater can't close. They're a big part of Sleighbell Springs or whatever."

"Look at you, so full of Christmas cheer," Jorge teases. "You feeling okay, Krampus?"

I roll my eyes. I may be a cynic living in a Christmas town, but that doesn't mean I want Sleighbell Springs to struggle. "Yeah, whatever. They're one of Ho Ho Handyman's best customers."

Jorge chuckles dryly from under the hood. "I'm sure this rant has nothing to do with the fact that Luck is strong-arming you into their show."

"Yeah, what the hell is that about?" I rise up again to pace the length of the hearse. Olive is on my heels, her nose nudging my hand for more pets. I scratch her ears as I walk. "They know I don't do dance shit anymore."

"You are a drag king, my guy." Jorge snorts. "A go-go dancer. You spend literally every weekend onstage *dancing*."

"Yeah, but the dancing I do there isn't for a recital!"

"What's the difference? Dancing is dancing." Jorge shrugs his wrench in my direction.

"It's not the same at all!" I sputter, struggling to articulate it to someone cis, who has never taken a single dance class. Who never felt the dysphoria with every leotard, tutu, or gendered routine. My mom put me in dance before I could read; I was surrounded by relentless hyperfemininity for fifteen years, unable to articulate why I hated the life I also loved more than anything. "The dancing I do now is for me, a way I can be myself. It's just me onstage, me and the audience who sees Felix."

"You really think Luck is going to make you be anyone but Felix?" Jorge asks, too gently, his brown eyes examining me under the curly black hair hanging in his face.

I swallow, because it sounds ridiculous when he says it. "No, but they want their dance co-captain. I can't be that person anymore. Not even for Luck."

"And Luck can?" Jorge turns back to the hearse. "They're not the same person anymore either. I know their transition stuff isn't quite the same as yours, but they felt trapped by the gender shit, too."

And doesn't that just strike a blow to my chest. The music from next door stops, and the garage echoes with quiet. "I wasn't trying to invalidate their gender identity or queerness—"

"Nah, man, I wasn't saying that at all." Jorge points his wrench at me. "You know I don't know the first thing about all that, and I sure as hell ain't getting into a debate or discussion about the whole trans discourse. I'm just saying, Luck teaches their classes differently, without all the rules about who can dance a certain way or wear bows or whatever. You might not hate it, especially since you don't even have to go to the class. You just have to do your usual drag shit."

As Luck tells their class what a great job they did today, I can feel my resolve weakening. "No, actually, it's not my usual drag shit," I mutter. "They want to do a burlesque number with me."

Jorge laughs, the sound echoing under the hood.

I groan. "I'm so glad my misfortune is funny to you."

He leans back, still cracking up as he looks at me, a wider smile on his face than I've seen in years. His headlamp shines in my eyes. "Bro! 'Misfortune'? You've probably had wet dreams about this. You poor friendzoned motherfucker!"

"Fuck off!" I shush him; if I can hear Luck, they can probably hear us. "Don't give me that gross friendzone bullshit. I am their friend, and always will be! If something was going to happen between us, it would have already."

There was one night, after a few too many wine coolers our senior year in high school, where I thought it might. But Luck immediately rejected me, which I understood and respected. We're friends, and that's enough. That'll always be enough.

Dancing with Luck was torture enough in high school, and that was mostly dance team and the occasional modern or tap number. I'd pulled away from ballet in middle school, Luck's favorite, citing the pointe shoes as an excuse. Now, we've both grown into who we really are. Rehearsing and performing with Luck now—seeing the layers of fabric slowly pull away to reveal their light brown skin, touching them in the way I've been wanting to for years, moving in sync together the way we did all those years ago—will be my own private temptation, leading me down the road to Hell.

"God damn it." I huff as the kids next door say goodbye to Luck, and the cars start to pull out of the parking lot.

"We all knew you were gonna do it, bro," Jorge chuckles, flicking his headlight off. "*You* just didn't know you were gonna do it yet."

Storming to the door that leads to the showroom-turned-dance atelier, I burst through into the bright, airy warmth of Luck's studio. I stalk along the carpeted edge of the room, careful not to track dirt onto the salvaged wood floors that were a pain in the ass to install and seal.

Wearing a skintight leotard and shorts that hug their curvy hips and thighs, their brown skin glowing with a sheen of sweat, Luck looks up at me. Their hands twist around the handle of the dry mop they're pushing across the studio floor, and their eyes are wide and hesitant, as if they're worried I'm about to let them down.

With a huff, I say, "Let's do this."

The beam on their face alone is already worth the emotional torture of the next few weeks. But Luck asked me for help, and I'll do anything for Luck's sake.

Four

Luck

"Felix, you are not going to regret this at all!" I beam, bouncing on the balls of my feet in excitement. I toss the dry mop down, the handle clattering on the carpeted seating area. "We're going to have so much fun!"

"I am already kind of regretting it," he grimaces, wrinkling his nose. "But fuck it, if it's for Twyla and Nisha."

"Right!" I nod, pang in my chest, even though he's probably also doing it for me, at least partly. Or more likely, for Jorge, who probably talked him into it for me. "So here's what I'm thinking! I already asked May if she'd emcee, so she'll introduce you as the first act, and use you as a demonstration for how to tip and cheer and all that stuff."

"Oh, okay, already got the boss lady roped into this too." Felix fusses with his coat, pulling his balaclava off. The studio is still warm from all the running around during the beginner tap class that just left. Warmer than Jorge keeps the garage, anyway. Felix's red curly mullet stays squished flat to his scalp, and my fingers itch to fluff the curls out. "I really had no choice in this, did I?"

I snort. "I mean, she's asking the rest of the cast for volunteers too, but she just assumed you would do it, yes." I trust May and Felix to get the crowd amped up and cheering more than anyone else in this town. They work well together onstage, as long as Felix doesn't have to talk. "She wants to do a bit with you where she interrupts your performance when they're not cheering enough, how they should tip, and so on. So the two of you have free reign to do whatever you want for that!"

"So, like every damn show at Sleigh Queen," Felix smirks, an amused twinkle in his blue eyes.

"Exactly!" I beam as the ideas keep spilling out of me, "Since the show is spring-themed, I thought it'd be fun to do something special for that. I'm thinking our number should be fun and campy, where we can get a little raunchy without it being too overtly sexual." I don't want to make Felix—or my brother—uncomfortable, after all. This is just a dance between two childhood friends. Even if we are stripping. "And modern was always our favorite back in the day, so we could put a contemporary twist to it! Estelle is already going to do an Easter Bunny number, and one of the lyra performers is doing a rite of spring, so that leaves Saint Patrick's Day open for us!" With an expectant smile, I pause, because I just know Felix will have something to say about that.

Felix groans. "You're suggesting what I think you're suggesting, aren't you?"

I giggle, delighted that he's putting up a fight. He agreed to May's idea too easily, which means he's taking this far too seriously. This may be a fundraiser, but it's still burlesque! And he's still Felix, stubborn, argumentative, but utterly sweet. With a smirk, I ask, "And what is it that you think I'm suggesting, cariño?"

"A leprechaun number? Really, Luck?" he groans, rubbing a hand over his face. "What are you going to be, a unicorn or some shit? A four-leaf clover?"

"A pot of gold at the end of the rainbow, naturally!" I pretend to toss my hair over my shoulder, even though my curls are pulled into a tight bun.

"Let me get this straight." Felix presses his hands together. He's so cute when he's this annoyed. "You want me, the short redhead trans guy, to dress as a *leprechaun* for your dance recital? That's offensive." He shakes his head, crossing his arms. "Not just offensive, it's a little transphobic."

With a scoff, I put my hand on my hip as I pop it. "Might I remind *you* that your drag name is Felix Navidad, and you are the furthest thing from Latino!"

He scoffs, pretending to be offended. "I asked Jorge before my first show as a drag king, and he said it was funny!"

Jealousy stirs in my gut as I fight to keep my smile bright. Three and a half years at Julliard, and I thought things would be the same in Sleighbell Springs forever. But no, I come back and Felix had not only transitioned, but he and my brother were closer than ever. Which is great. Really! Felix was so much happier and confident, and Jorge needed a friend after the accident. I didn't mind at all that my best friend replaced me with my brother, in every sense of our relationship. No, I wasn't hurt at all that Felix was the first person I'd come out to as genderqueer, but my brother got to be the first to hear about Felix's drag persona that eventually became his name. I didn't even know Felix was doing drag at all until I came back for Christmas, or that he was transitioning until Jorge told me not to use his deadname anymore. I wasn't part of any of Felix's transition, the way I invited him to be a part of mine.

"Of course he did!" I roll my eyes, my hurt winning out over my determination to be cheerful. "You could tell Jorge to drink his own piss, and he would! He'll agree to anything for you!"

Felix whistles. "Damn, is Jorge into—"

"Not the point!" I interrupt, crossing my arms to hide my heartache. I really don't like thinking about my brother and Felix's mutual pining, but especially not any potential piss kinks. Even though I'm pretty sure Felix is joking, and I wouldn't judge him or my brother if they were into that. Just as long as they leave me out of it. The less I see of their inevitable relationship, the happier I can be for them. "The point is, Reddit told me it was fine, so it's not offensive!"

"Oh, if *Reddit* says so," Felix snarks, but his face falls ever so slightly. I lean forward to hear what he's about to say, because that is his serious discussion face. "All the same, you were right earlier. That I love dancing, and performing, but..." He groans. "Look, the idea of dancing in a recital brings me right back to high school, and all the gross dysphoric feelings that come with it."

"Oh." I swallow. "I didn't realize."

I had many of the same feelings, back then. We loved dancing, had our whole lives. However, we also confided in each other about all the things that poisoned it—supporting each other through all those weird, confusing emotions we didn't have the words for yet. In college, I'd learned to connect dance to my newfound gender expression, the queerness inside of me, instead of the rules and restrictions of our childhood dance teachers. I found masculinity and gender fuckery could thrive in ballet, in tap, in modern, just as easily as the hyperfemininity I'd been forced to portray my whole life.

But the Kellys couldn't afford Julliard, or sending their eldest kid anywhere out of state. Felix went to a construction-focused trade program in the next town over, got certified in contract work to help out with Ho Ho Handyman. He reconnected with dance by becoming Felix Navidad at Sleigh Queen on the weekends, where he'd discovered his trans identity too.

Felix sighs. "I guess I'm feeling weird about the idea of doing a dance recital, even though I know it's for a good cause. I just...I left that behind when I transitioned, and I'm not loving the idea of us returning to our high school dance team roles again."

"Then we won't," I say simply.

He looks up at me. "But you wanted the fundraiser—"

"Oh, we're still doing the number, cariño, don't doubt it!" I poke his nose, the way he hates. His face scrunches up in displeasure, but Felix doesn't pull away. "But we aren't doing it as former co-captains reliving our former glory. We're Luck and Felix now, and this is no mere dance recital."

Felix frowns. "Pretty sure it is. You taught a dance class, the dance class is performing. That's a dance recital."

"No, it's a burlesque performance!" I smirk. "No, we're not simply dancing, Felix, or showcasing what moves we learned. We're stripping."

Felix's face goes into that too-composed mask, his jaw tight. But his cheeks redden ever so slightly.

I lean in, tugging down the zipper of his coat ever so slowly as I murmur, "I want you to chase me around the stage, while I'm in a sexy rainbow dress that leaves almost nothing to the imagination. I want you to pull it off of me, color by color, until all I'm wearing is gold pasties, a thong, and body glitter." I smirk, eyeing him up and down, overly flirtatious so he knows I'm not *actually* coming onto him. "And I want you in a teeny tiny pair of shorts with a campy belt buckle that's so big, it's obscene, bending over to show all of Sleighbell Springs that tight little ass of yours." As the zipper of his coat pops apart, I glance up at him; his ears are as red as his hair where it peeks out from his cap. "While they shower us with money."

His swallow is audible. "Can I pick it up? The money, I mean."

My smile is victorious, because I have him. I've known this man since we were five, and I know exactly what gets Felix going. Though when we were kids, he was more into playing wolves and buying candy, than being a slutty little exhibitionist, but we've all changed over the years. "Felix, I want you to bend that cute butt over, all night long, in front of everyone in Sleighbell Springs. The adults, anyway."

Felix sucks in a breath so fast, it almost sounds like a gasp, and *oh*, my heart pounds at the sound. "You mean...I can be the bendover boy?"

"For the whole goddamn show, Felix," I breathe. "That's why I want you to do the opening act."

"Fuck, I *love* being the bendover boy." He practically growls as he says it. The sound resonates through my whole body like an electric shock.

"I know you do, cariño." I pat his chest, stepping back before my feelings get carried away. I turn on my heel, making a beeline to where my phone is plugged into the sound system in the corner. "So, should we run through the choreography I have planned? I'm still working on it, but I have the main beats down, so we can fill it in as we go, like we used to, right?" My voice is too bright, but I don't care. I need space.

"Do you have clothes?" Felix asks. I look over my shoulder right when he slides the straps of his unzipped work overalls down his arms. The canvas falls away to reveal the built chest under his flannel shirt. His coat is in a puddle on the carpet behind him. "I wasn't expecting to dance, so I didn't bring anything to wear."

"Uh..." I blink, fascinated by the patch of chest hair peeking out from the vee in his shirt as he unbuttons it. Gender envy, that's all this is. I'm not drooling. Or wishing he'd slow down to let me savor the sight of him, exposing the lines of his neck and curve of his pecs under his tank top with each undone button.

The door to the garage banging open makes us both jump.

"I'm taking— Oh!" Jorge looks between us, then raises his eyebrows at Felix, frozen and halfway through taking his shirt off. Cheeks bright red, Felix wraps the fabric back over his chest. "I was coming to tell you I'm taking off, but it looks like Felix is doing the same thing."

Felix huffs. "I will beat your ass so hard, dude!"

"Welp, bye! See you at home, hermane!" Jorge finger guns as he backs through the door. Olive circles his feet as he moves. "I was never here, never saw anything!"

"We're just dancing!" I call after him, guilt writhing in my gut. How could I possibly be drooling over Felix, knowing Jorge was on the other side of the door? As if he doesn't have enough internalized shit to work through, without me checking out the person he's had a crush on since high school?! "You know, maybe you're right. I have some spare clothes, but it's late." I nod. That's a perfectly reasonable excuse to abort mission. "I'll text you my schedule, and you find a time that works for you for us to start rehearsing together, okay?"

Felix is already shrugging his coveralls back on, his flannel still unbuttoned dangerously low. "Yeah, that works. I should probably focus on repairing the roof the next couple days, anyway. I got some plywood over it, but that's not going to keep the weather out. Maybe Saturday?"

I nod, too emphatically. "Yup! Yes! Great! We're doing a costume workshop Saturday morning, and then some open practice time. Maybe while they're working on their numbers, we can start on ours?"

He nods. "Do you want a ride home?"

"Oh, no, thank you!" I demure, ushering him out the door. Felix already knows I'll say no, and honestly, I need to ride off this energy, this guilt, and this surge of desire that sprang up out of nowhere. "You get home safe!"

Felix halts, halfway through the door. "Text me when you do, okay?" His blue eyes dig into mine, insisting on a response, to make sure I know he's serious.

Heart in my throat, I nod, pretending that one small act of concern isn't everything to me. I wave goodbye as the door shuts behind him, before pressing my hand to my chest.

I'm not allowed to want Felix. I got over my crush in high school when I found out Jorge liked him, and I've kept it at bay for this long. Felix and I are friends. Best friends! He and my brother are meant for each other, eventually when they're ready, and I would never get in the way of that.

A few weeks of sensual dancing with my bestie—my sweet, generous, incredibly hot bestie—will be a mere blip on the radar!

Five

Luck

By the time Saturday morning rolls around, I almost convince myself that I've forgotten I invited Felix to Dancers and Prancers for open studio. Have I scolded myself for how unreasonably nervous I am to dance with him again? Nope! Not once! Have I caught myself daydreaming about what might have happened if Jorge hadn't come in? Absolutely not! Do I wish we were dancing together for the first time in private, instead of whoever happens to be in the studio when he comes? Yes, but as much as I want to trust myself, perhaps it's best to have an audience.

Our burlesque class meets on Sunday nights, but I've always left the schedule open on weekend mornings for whoever in Sleighbell Springs needs floor time, so long as they're respectful of everyone else there. Since we've started rehearsing our solos for the recital, the burlesque folks take over a back corner, leaving the barre for the ballerinas. Instead of using the mirror, we practice our crowdwork and give each other audience feedback. Even with most of our clothes staying on, the communal environment has been invaluable.

Safer for my mirror wall too, to have everyone in this active group far away from any risk of breaking one; I cannot afford any more bad luck right now. However, our group is so raucous that most of the dancers who are regulars at open studio have started to come on Sunday mornings, instead of Saturdays now. I'd feel bad, but there's only a few weeks left.

The group of trans mascs are running through their choreo (a hair metal performance a la Kiss) to some song I've never heard of before. Nome, the ringleader who convinced the group to sign up for this class, insists it's a classic.

I'm not sure how to give them feedback. Or if I should. Their routine is solid, but the energy is...off somehow. Keiran keeps tripping over his feet during transitions, or Aiden will get distracted by the ad-lib moves they throw in and fall half a step behind. Avery needs to move bigger, to fit the music.

In my professional opinion, it's not working. Maybe I'm just judgy because I think the song is a poor fit. However, it's their solo, and I've been encouraging everyone to do solos that make them feel their best, not necessarily what makes good burlesque.

"Watch your mark!" I call, too late. I wince as Avery and Nome smack into each other mid-spin.

"You're supposed to go the other way!" Nome rubs xis bicep.

"Sorry!" Avery covers their mouth, eyes wide. "Are you okay?"

"Yeah, but dang, you have sharp elbows!" Xe teases. "Should we take it from the top?"

The others agree, and I return to gluing gold rhinestones onto a pasty, keeping one eye on their still-stiff performance.

"That better not be for me," a raspy voice mutters, right in my ear.

I jump, smearing glue on my fingers. A backpack drops next to me with a heavy thud and a metallic clank, and I drop the glue entirely, the bottle clattering to the floor. Thankfully, on the carpeted edge of the studio, instead of my immaculate wood floors.

Felix shrugs off his coat, dropping it on the ground next to his bag.

A peek of bare skin under his flannel, just along his hip, makes me sputter a string of incoherent words. Even I don't know what I'm trying to say. The only clear word is "mine."

"What?" Felix asks, kneeling next to me. His hunter green joggers are tight around his thick thighs.

"Mine," I repeat, holding out the half-finished pasty. "This is mine. I have big areolas."

Giggles from Aaron and Junie next to me are quickly muffled, and Felix's face flushes pink. "Oh. Okay..."

"Sorry, TMI!" My cheeks are burning hot. I can feel everyone's eyes looking at us. "Just explaining it's for me, not you." I put the pasty down. Maybe the floor will open up and swallow me whole. "I have some for you, though!" I hand him some green sequined four-leaf clovers I decorated earlier this week.

"Cute, but I don't need them?" Felix explains hesitantly, as if he's confused.

"Oh, you don't have to wear them!" I blurt out. Maybe I should take a vow of silence for the rest of my life. "Just thought they would be fun!"

"They are!" Felix insists. "I just...I have my own gear?" He unzips his bag, pulling out a green leather harness. "This usually covers where my nips used to be. Plus, uh...chest hair and adhesive doesn't really mix well."

"Where they used to be?" Nome asks, xis group's routine completely interrupted by Felix's presence. "You don't have nips? Like none?" Xis jaw hangs open. "That's so cool!"

Felix jumps, as if he had forgotten the rest of the class was listening. "Oh, uh, no? I didn't really want to keep them, so I didn't."

"Can I see?" Keiran asks, crossing his arms to minimize his own bound chest. "And all the stuff you brought? We've been struggling with what to wear for this. All we know is we want tearaway pants, but with hair metal, they wore a lot of tight pants, and all of our prototypes tear open too early."

"But if we let them out, the pleather looks saggy," Nome explains. "Nobody likes saggy pleather."

Felix nods knowingly, unbuttoning his flannel.

Looking determinedly away, I frown. "How um...committed to hair metal are all of you?"

"I mean, our performance is in two weeks..." Keiran shrugs. "Kinda late to change it."

"Dance can surprise you with how flexible it can be." I tilt my head, unconvinced I should be saying anything, but I can't take it anymore. I hate telling people what to do, but the song is all wrong. Besides, Felix is here now, and he loves being a jerk. This might be my chance; he'll back me up, I'm sure. "The choreo is great, but it might fit another genre better?"

The trans masc crew exchanges looks, deferring to Nome, who shrugs again. Xe clears xis throat. "What did you have in mind?"

I shake my head, still wanting them to have some autonomy in the decision. "Nothing in particular, but it might be worth exploring."

"Can I see it?" Felix asks, pulling his undershirt off. "The routine?"

There's no avoiding it this time. Neither hell nor high water could drag my eyes from the chiseled chest, the coat of curly red hair dusting his pale, freckled skin, the trail that darkens on its journey down into his joggers, highlighting every defined abdominal muscle and the cut of his hips. I want to lick the crease, kiss every mole, feel each of those solid muscles move underneath me. Preferably with my thighs.

An elbow to my ribs makes me jump; my body and nerves are ablaze, quivering under my skin. "Babe, close your mouth before you drool all over the floor," Junie teases in my ear. "Should I go get a mop for when you stand up?"

"Junie!" I protest, but she's got a point. My pussy is blooming between my legs, just as thirsty as the rest of me. I rub my eyes. Oh, this is bad!

As the music starts again, Felix pulls the leather harness over his head, tugging the straps tight against his skin. The clink of the buckle is still audible over the squeal of the guitar. The green leather spans the breadth of his wide chest, a set of o-rings framing his pecs. Between the hair and the leather, there's no sign that he no longer has nipples. Just the faded lines of his scars curve along his ribs.

A hand turns my chin toward the dance floor, and pretends to wipe some drool from my lip. Aaron winks as he walks by, running a hand along Felix's chest with a "hey, Daddy!" He circles Felix, smirking as he admires him.

"No," Felix shakes his head, his cheeks pink. "Aaron, we've been over this. I am not your Daddy, or anyone's daddy."

"I'm not flirting with you, babe. We all know you're off the market," Aaron smiles sympathetically at me from over Felix's shoulder. My heart drops; am I so obvious? How could I forget about Jorge's feelings, just like that? "Just thought you might want to actually watch the performance you're supposed to be analyzing."

"I am!" Felix swats Aaron's hand from creeping up his chest. Aaron catches it and holds tight to Felix's hand with a familiarity that makes me wonder if I should be worried about what Jorge might see at Sleigh Queen, if he ever went to see his crush's performances. I don't often go myself; Felix is a different person when he's onstage, and it leaves me feeling strange. Like I don't know him as well as I think I do. Like perhaps there's this side of him I used to know, and no longer do. Like his drag family has replaced the connection we used to have. It all leaves me unreasonably jealous, because I never thought we'd ever grow apart.

With a swallow and a chill crossing my skin, I focus on the rehearsing group of four genderful folks. They are nailing every beat, bringing the campy, sexual energy...but something about it is falling flat.

Felix squats next to me, his brow furrowed the way it used to when we would watch the team we captained together. "Yeah, the song is wrong," he murmurs.

I nod, whispering, "I think the whole genre is wrong. The choreo is good, but something about the vibe isn't hitting."

Felix hums in agreement. "This needs to be pop."

"It needs to be something campy, and a guy singing though, for gender affirming reasons," I murmur quietly. "There are not many campy guy pop songs that are this tempo."

"What about a boy band?" Felix returns. "Something '90s or early 2000s, for the camp factor."

"Hanson? An Mmmbop moment?"

"Too childish. New Kids on the Block?" Felix smirks.

I smile, nostalgic for how we used to brainstorm together, exactly like this. No wrong ideas, just riffing on each other's thoughts until the final answer coalesced into being between us. We used to be so in sync. I gasp, "N*Sync!"

"There's only four of them," he points out.

"You're so persnickety. New Kids on the Block has five too!" I roll my eyes. "So what if there's only four of them? They can just skip Just—" I gasp again.

"What?" Felix asks, trepidation audible.

My smile grows mischievous the longer I look at him.

"No!" Felix waves a hand. "Nope! You said two numbers."

"What's the harm in one more?" I jump up, tugging on his arm. When Felix doesn't stand, I frown, hooking a finger through the center o-ring to pull him along. Felix doesn't protest as much as I expect him to as he stumbles along behind me.

Aaron whistles. "Now bark, Daddy!"

"Fuck off!" Felix grumbles over his shoulder.

I reposition the group shoulder to shoulder, Felix next to Keiran on the end, so he can follow along with the choreo. "Your solos will be a little shorter, so improvise a bit with the song when it's your turn." I turn around to beam at the rest of the class. "Imagine these handsome fellas in white suits. Ooh, maybe fedoras?"

"Backstreet Boys!" Junie practically screams. "Oh my god, Felix is the perfect Brian!"

"Sorry, bro," Nome pats Felix's shoulder. "Harness looks hot, though!"

"Thanks," Felix sighs.

"I'll get you a Sexy Santas sweatshirt tomorrow during class," Aiden says. "And teach you the secret handshake."

Felix's face freezes, visibly trying not to be rude to his new troupe-mates, who are all trans masc and younger than him. Hell, I'm pretty sure he used to babysit half of them. While Felix may be a grump, he is also incredibly kind. Conflict wars in his eyes as he fights to keep from teasing me relentlessly for the cheesy class name, because it would also mean teasing the trans youth who might take it personally. "What have you gotten me into?" he mouths behind Keiran's back. "Sexy Santas? Really?"

With a wink, I find the song on my playlist, and gleefully hit play. "Larger Than Life" starts over the sound system.

"Are we lip-syncing?" Felix asks, following Keiran's footwork. Typical of Felix, he catches on within moments, as if he's been practicing for weeks.

"No," Nome responds from the center, nailing the first body roll with a smirk and a touch of a shoulder lean that hadn't emerged with the old song.

Junie and I both cheer.

"Should we, though?" Avery asks from the opposite end of Felix. "I know all the words. I don't think I'll be able to stop myself."

"Let's do it, then!" Aiden, normally the quietest one in class, grapevines to the center for his solo. He's not shy, or timid the way Avery can be. Just a trans man of few words, expressing himself through intentionally ugly sweatshirts.

They all jump right into lip-syncing, quietly bickering about who gets to be who, but each of them ends their solos at a natural pause in the song, stripping during the choruses. Felix rolls along with it, catching onto the choreo and pretending to whip his pants off when they do at the end of the bridge, just before going into his own improvised solo.

It's so...right, seeing Felix like this. In his element, quietly directing the other guys in his grumpy but kind way. Just like he used to be with our team, and yet, so incredibly different. I bite my lip, throat tightening a little at the surge of affection.

They all high-five each other as the song finishes. Nome grins at me. "Yeah, you were right, the song needed changing. That felt great!"

"Good! I knew we'd find the right fit!" I beam. Of course I was right. I always am!

"We'll need new outfits, but the Millennium era was nice and boxy," Keiran says with an approving nod, reattaching his pants around his hips. "Junie, can you help us adjust the pattern?"

"Already on it!" Junie gives a thumbs-up from the back of the room. As a semi-professional cosplayer, she's the go-to seamstress and tailor for our *Nutcracker* production, and makes a lot of the costumes in town. Her expertise has been invaluable for crafting a collection of outfits that can quickly and sexily come off.

"Can we see the number you guys are doing?" Avery asks me.

Felix and I exchange a trepidacious look. I wave a hand. "Oh, we don't really have anything planned quite yet."

"But you have ideas, right?" Estelle prompts, casually en point in the back of the room with her fans spread behind her. "Can we see your creative process?"

Felix gives me a subtle nod.

"So," I step onto the hardwood, pacing around the space, "I want to subvert expectations. Start off with something campy and fun and goofy, since we'll have cheesy outfits on." Felix matches my pacing, circling opposite me on the floor. I do a quick spin and skip away, just before he reaches me. "But then the music shifts, and it ends up being a bit heavy and sensual and hits people right in the heart." When I stop short to turn again, he collides into me.

"Sorry!" Felix mutters, catching me before I can even begin to fall over. "I thought I was chasing you."

"You are! Sorry!" I grimace in apology, stepping out of the strong grip supporting my biceps. "It's not like you can read my mind, or hear the music in it. I should have hinted I was about to stop."

"What's the music?" Junie asks. "I wanna hear!"

"Well, since it's St. Patrick's Day themed, I was thinking it'd start off with some fun fiddle tune—"

"St. Patrick's Day?" Aaron screams. "Are you dressing our short king as a leprechaun!?"

I grin at Felix's groan. "Sure am! And I am the rainbow he's chasing, only as he pulls off the colors, one by one, I'm revealed to be the pot of gold he's been looking for the whole show." I pose with a flourish of my hands and shimmy. "Well, the whole first half! I figure our number will be right before intermission, and then we can put May as the finale for the second act. The setlist isn't finalized yet."

"Let's see it!" Junie calls.

"How do you feel about Hozier?" I ask Felix quietly, waiting for his shrug before skipping to my phone to play a "Francesca" remix that I already had my little brother Efrain put together. I knew Felix wouldn't care, and Efrain is always so helpful and considerate, even when he's busy with baseball season at UConn. He's the real sweetheart of the family.

"So, I'm picturing we'll have this fun little fiddle remix playing, while Felix is picking up the dollars and stripper droppings for the act before ours," I say as I put Felix on one side of the floor, and scurry over to the other side while the fiddle music plays. "And then he'll be admiring me from across the stage, and the music will drop into this." I cue a drop in the beat at the perfect time stamp, and turn to face him, starting that same traveling circle we were playing with a moment ago. "And from there, we have two verses, two choruses and an outro to get me naked."

Felix's eyes don't leave me as he paces, matching my speed. He seems almost cautious.

"We can play with the silk scarves that will make up my dress, make it a little kinky!" I shimmy, to Junie and Aaron's cheers. "And tease an almost-kiss moment or two," I glance coquettishly over my shoulder, waiting for Felix to get closer and closer, until he's close enough to touch. I leap out of the way when he reaches out for me, pirouetting across the room, with a teasing grin once I come to a stop and tear my eyes away from my spot. "Until finally, you realize what a treasure I am, and I let you catch me."

Felix is watching me, carefully following my lead. So carefully that he's not taking any initiative of his own. I frown, pausing, nodding for him to do what felt right, to listen to the instincts I trust more than my own.

But he doesn't. He seems almost stiff, uncomfortable.

"You okay?" I mouth to him.

Felix nods. The slow build from the verse overflows into the chorus, adding a little swagger to his pursuit with some turns.

"No, come closer!" I point at a spot on the ground about three feet further. "How are you supposed to pull my clothes off if you're so far away?"

"I don't want to catch you too early!" he argues, jaw tightening as he runs a hand through his curly red mullet.

"You won't! Just give me something to work with, let me tease you a little!" I cross my arms. We've already missed the whole second verse. There is a lot of work ahead of us if we can't even find the chemistry while improvising this. "You know, let's skip ahead. Let's pretend you just pulled the last color from me, and I'm all bashful and hiding, and you stop chasing." I scurry over to Junie and pull her scarf off the back of her chair. "Here, pretend to catch me. Remember, you can make it a little racy."

Instead of lassoing me with the scarf, like I expect, Felix wraps it around his wrists and sinks to his knees.

As he looks up at me, I freeze, breath catching in my throat at how wide his eyes go.

Oh.

Like a supplicant, Felix crawls toward me in long glides along the hardwood floor. His blue eyes won't let go of mine as he comes closer and closer.

Oh. *Oh*... Why is it so warm in here?

Trying to catch my breath, I take a tentative step toward him. I use the scarf to pull him up to his feet, ducking under his arms so he's holding me from behind. The scarf covers my chest as he unravels it from around his wrists. Every inch of him burns hot against my back, the roughness of his chest hair against my bare shoulders. The cool metal of the o-ring against my spine sends a shudder through me.

Heart pounding, I attempt a pirouette within the circle of his arms, and—just like I hoped for—he catches me around the thigh, bringing me into a dip with so much tenderness, I can't breathe.

Just as the song ends, I remember to wrap the scarf from around my chest and wrap it around his neck, exposing what will eventually be my mostly naked body, as the last measures fade into nothing.

We hold the pose for longer than I expect. I'm not thin by most standards, and especially not ballet standards. I love my curves, my generous thighs and soft belly, but they weren't there the last time Felix and I danced together.

Felix's arms don't tremble in the slightest; his knee propped under the small of my back barely supports any weight. Instead, his blue eyes hold my gaze just as steadily as his muscular arms hold my body, stealing my breath with the intensity emanating from him. Heat radiates from his eyes as much as his body.

It's the slow clap from our audience that builds to cheers and whoops that makes us jump apart.

"Sorry," Felix fiddles with his harness. "We need to work on that."

"Yeah, but it's a great first run!" My voice is breathless as I attempt my normal cheer. The next two weeks are about to be torture. Why am I doing this to myself?

Felix nods, unbuckling his harness. "I should go. I have to uh, work on the theater? Yeah. Theater. Gotta go." He waves a hand goodbye, but doesn't leave. "Insurance guy is coming on Monday, so Twyla wanted to get my opinion before he does his inspection so she knows what to ask for."

"Right!" I nod. "Well, thanks for coming! I hope you had fun?"

"Yeah." Felix pulls the harness off, avoiding looking at me just as hard as I'm staring at him. I follow him to the edge of the floor, where his backpack is still open. He pulls his flannel on without his undershirt, buttoning it frantically. "I gotta go. Twyla. Theater."

"Yup!" My jaw hurt from faking this smile. My eyes ache with how hard I'm *not* looking at that peek of chest hair from the vee of his shirt. "Byeeee!"

Still in his dance shoes, Felix grabs his coat and shoves his feet into his boots, then runs out the door.

Breaking the silence, Aaron whistles slowly. "Damn."

Once again remembering the class is here and watching all of my humiliation, I groan. "Was it that bad?"

"The dance? I have no idea!" Aaron laughs, fanning himself. "God, what I wouldn't give for him to kneel like that for me! I am just a hole, sir!"

"Hot, bossy, *and* he can dance?" Junie eyes me up and down. "You really are lucky!"

"It's just a dance!" I mutter, turning away from them and stalking toward the bathroom. Embarrassment burns hotter than my arousal as it sinks in how much I just humiliated myself.

Splashing my face with cold water brings me back to my senses. "Fuck," I groan as I look at myself in the mirror. My nose is red from how flushed I am. "Jorge cannot hear about this."

My brother is still so fragile, even after all these years. On the outside, he's healed from the accident. But neither of us has grieved the way the twins did years ago. The way my titi did when she had to step up and be the executor for my parent's estate.

All these years, Jorge and I have both simply...managed. While this is my year of reclaiming my life, I don't know that Jorge is there yet. I have to put him first; his heart might not recover if he finds out I've been thirsting after the person he's loved for decades, the person who has been his closest confidant since I moved to New York, the person who has always been there for him.

My brother can never know this means anything more than a dance to me. He especially cannot know how Felix crawling toward me lit every nerve in my body on fire, how right I felt in his arms. Or how tempted I was to tug on that scarf, to bring his mouth down the few scant inches to mine.

No, Jorge can never get the idea that this could ever mean more than a favor. For me, or for Felix. I may lie to myself constantly, but I know Felix better than anyone, and there was desire in his eyes, too.

Six

Felix

"Ingrid, please!" I plead, clasping my hands together. "You're my second to last hope!"

Ingrid Frostbender, the owner of Frostbender Orchard and Tree farm, shakes her head. Muscular arms, clad in a flannel so soft-looking that I'm tempted to ask where she got it, fold over her chest as she leans against the barn door. The evergreens surrounding us fill the crisp spring air with a sweet smell from the sap. "Felix, I don't know why you bothered asking. We don't even have any lumber ready to go, let alone sheet metal."

"But I'm desperate," I sigh, my gut sinking.

She tsks sympathetically. "The hardware store not have anything in stock?"

In lieu of the truth, I shake my head. "They placed an order for me, but that's for the permanent renovations once the insurance money comes through. I need something a bit more weatherproof than plywood in the meantime."

The adjuster the insurance company sent over was full of shit, ignoring Twyla and Nisha completely, and arguing with me about everything. But we managed to get permission to reopen the theater for the fundraiser, on the condition that I patch the roof with something more permanent than the scrapwood and tarp I used to block the elements.

"Is the damage bad?" Ingrid asks, too casually, tugging on the end of her ash brown braid.

I shake my head. Everyone in this town is so damn nosy; this is the fifth person today to ask me about the condition of the theater. At this point, I could replay my answer in my sleep. "The insurance guy thinks there was a gap in the pitchwork that slowly wore a crack from the freeze thaw cycle. There are a couple other spots that need work, but structurally, the roof is sound, other than the three foot hole that just went through yet another heavy snowstorm this year. The beams and structure are still solid, just need to get the special order in for the materials, since it's a historic building."

Ingrid nods, which for her, is basically a smile at the good news. "Wish I had something for you, but all I got this time of year is mulch and green lumber."

I nod back. "I get it. I'll just..." I groan, "ask Paul Wilson, I guess."

Ingrid wrinkles her nose. "Desperate times, huh? Good luck!"

With a shrug, I scoff. "It needs to be done."

Back in my truck, I pull out my phone before driving away from the tree farm, cursing under my breath the whole time. I hate begging. Everyone—well, almost everyone—in Sleighbell Springs is nice enough to give a stranger the shirt off their back. But they've bent over backwards for Dad for decades, and even the nicest residents have their limits with Ho Ho Handyman's unpaid debts.

Melvin at the hardware store was generous enough to place an order for me without taking payment. However, I won't see a single washer or screw from that until Twyla and Nisha's insurance check comes, unless this fundraiser of Luck's is wildly successful. Dad has dozens of overdue invoices, and as his "employee" (I scoff, because employees get paid), I have to use the Ho Ho Handyman account.

The lumberyard in the next town over is less generous, not even letting me in the yard unless I settle Dad's debt with them first. Any credit, financial or social, that Dad might have had dried up long ago, sucked bone dry with lotto tickets and twenty-four packs of beer.

But Luck is counting on me to get the theater in good enough shape to reopen.

Agreeing to this was a mistake. All of it. None more than the dance. Especially after how thrown off and unsettled Luck was when I let my mask slip the other day, when I almost kissed them. In front of everyone!

Forget almost kissing them; I fucking crawled across the floor for them at the slightest urging. Have I no dignity? I groan out a laugh, banging my forehead on the steering wheel. As far as Luck is concerned, my dignity is meaningless. But they weren't supposed to know that. Luck doesn't want me to want them. They have made that clear for years.

The awkwardness of last night's class made that even more abundantly clear. Shame curdling my gut, I force out the text.

> Hey, could let your uncle know I'm coming to see him?

Their response is immediate.

> No, Felix! Do NOT go to Paul!

> I need to. No one else in town has sheet metal.

> Correction: Melvin *has* sheet metal, but I can't afford it.

> Bleghiorfjgoirjgoirjg I would get it to you in a heartbeat, but I barely have enough for Luis and Efrain's tuition this month. I'll see what I can do.

I lean back to wait. No point in driving until I get confirmation that Luck's uncle knows I'll be coming his way. I sure as hell am not risking showing up without warning. I value my life.

Twyla and Nisha confided in me that unless the insurance money comes through within a month or two, they might not be able to stay open. They barely had a cushion after the busy season, and it's a long time before the tourists come back. I'm just fortunate that the insurance adjuster didn't look too closely at my qualifications to make this repair. I have the personal certifications, but Ho Ho Handyman certainly doesn't. I'm not even sure Dad remembered to renew his contractor's license last year. But since I've been approved to make the repair, then I'll do what I can to make this affordable for Luck's friends.

And get through this damn performance to raise as much as Sleighbell Springs can.

Just the memory of that first rehearsal two days ago leaves me flushed hot under my coveralls. After the exquisite torture of Saturday—having Luck's eyes on me, their lips parted as they drank in my body, the feel of them in my arms, the tug of their finger through my harness, the hardwood against my knees as I crawled toward them—

The phone buzzing in my hand snaps me out of my fantasy. But it's not Luck texting me; Rudy's calling.

"The fuck do you want?" I ask when I pick up.

"Some hello!" I can practically hear my snotty younger brother roll his eyes. "Can you come get me?"

With a resigned sigh, I put the truck in drive. "Why and where are you?"

"Your lover boy's garage," Rudy teases in a singsong. "My truck was making a weird noise, so Jorge is taking a look for me, but he hates me, so it's awkward, and I wanna go home instead of standing here while he glowers at me."

"How are you planning on paying him?" I ask.

"IOU til payday?" Rudy says it like a question.

In the background, Jorge mutters a "Yeah, whatever, jackass."

"Stop taking advantage of Jorge, dickwad!" I grumble. "I'll be there in ten, but you're going to help me until he's done with your car." I pause, then add, "I need you as a witness when I stop by Paul's."

"We're going to Paul's?" Rudy groans, and Jorge curses in the background at his uncle's name.

"Yup! Bye!" I hang up the phone before they can talk me out of it.

Luck has texted me back by the time I get to Dancers and Prancers:

> Uncle Paul is aware that you are on your way and in need of sheet metal. Good luck!

> Also, I might come to the show at Sleigh Queen on Saturday, for my day-after-my-birthday celebration? Is that okay?

> I feel like we made a lot of progress yesterday, but I want to study you in your element, the sexy hot Felix you are now! So we can truly connect as dance partners again.

With a slow sigh, I am transported to the misery of *yesterday's* class. I'd gotten there a bit early, so we could figure out the choreography in private, without an audience to witness my insatiable longing for my best friend. We managed to get through the routine with an idea of what we were doing, but we were still so awkward, stiff— No, *I* was so awkward and stiff. Luck was simply frustrated with how awkward and stiff I was.

And I was just as frustrated, increasingly so as Luck left me to rehearse for the other number they voluntold me for, the damn boy band number. Funny how easily I can dance with these young trans kids, but not my best friend. I'd watched as Luck rehearsed their group numbers, drinking in the arch of their back as they stretched forward like a kitten during WAP, each ripple through their thick thighs and ass as their hips bounced up and down against the floor.

How can I be anything but awkward and stiff, when I don't want to just dance with them? When kneeling for them was the single most holy experience I've ever had? When I want my face buried between those thighs? When I've convinced myself the attraction in Luck's eyes for my body wasn't solely in my head? It doesn't mean that they can return the feelings I've been consumed by since we were teenagers. But the way they looked at me, I still...hope.

The passenger door pops open, and Olive bounds in to lick my face, followed by Jorge. "I'm not letting you visit Paul alone," Jorge says instead of a greeting as he pulls himself into the cab, adjusting his leg with a wince.

"Can't keep you lover boys apart for a minute!" Rudy shoves Jorge over to the middle seat, leaving me crushed by Olive, with a face full of fur. Her tongue lolls to the side as she pants directly in my ear.

"You just can't shut the fuck up about that lover boy shit, can you?" Jorge grumbles, hauling his leg over the gear shift. As Olive settles into his lap, I adjust my foot as best I can, giving him room to stretch out. Rudy's such an ass for making the taller guy with chronic pain sit in the middle. But I'd rather sit next to Jorge than my brother.

"Can you two just stop bickering while you're in my truck?" I craft a quick response to Luck, before I pull out of the parking lot and toward the edge of town. "I already don't want *any* of you in my truck with me—sorry, Olive, not even you—the least you can do is shut up."

> Yeah, of course. And thank you. I know how much it costs for you to text him, but I wouldn't have asked if I had any other option.

> I know. <3 Text me if he gives you any trouble.

"WELL, WELL, LOOK WHO it is," Paul Wilson folds his arm over his chest as we all pile out of the truck. He stands on his front step with his wife Lydia, Luck and Jorge's titi. "Thought I'd seen the last of you on my property after last time."

Ignoring him, I open up the truck bed. It's really a relief to have Jorge and Rudy here with me; their tempers are much cooler than mine, and I loathe this man on a good day. The Wilson's yard, on the edge of town in a neighborhood where the tourists rarely go, is full of junk. Under the melting snow, tires, a box spring, and a toilet all decorate the front lawn. And that's just what's visible this time of year. Even in the cold spring air, the smell of dust, must, and rust surrounds their home.

I will never understand why anyone in this town gives Paul Wilson the time of day. He's a shit neighbor, keeping his yard junky on purpose to keep the property value on his block down in his attempt to buy everyone out. He's a scammy realtor, basically operating a triangle scheme of an agency. And for some reason, people put up with him. Probably because he's the head of the business approval committee on the Chamber of Holiday Cheer, and anyone starting a company in this town depends on his blessing.

Lydia Wilson, other than her poor choice of husband, is nice enough. But I haven't voluntarily shared breathing air with this sorry excuse for a man in years.

However, there's bound to be some scrap metal buried under the snow. It might be cheap and rusty, but it'll last until the insurance check comes in.

Luckily, Jorge takes over the conversation, greeting his titi with a hug and a kiss on the cheek, and a nod for Paul, explaining what we need. I'm happy to be ignored, not trusting what I might say to this man.

Olive, normally on Jorge's heels at all times, waits in the car. Paul makes her so anxious that she curls up on the floor of the passenger seat, instead of jumping out of the truck and greeting everyone with her usual wiggles and kisses.

Ignoring me and Rudy completely, Paul leads the way to a dilapidated shed in the backyard. The pickings are slim in the cluttered and dingy space, but Rudy and I manage to find enough corrugated tin that looks like it's seen better days, some lumber that I don't even need to sight to tell it's warped, and an ancient but unopened tube of sealant, among some other odds and ends. Enough to get the job done, at least until after the show, when I can hopefully use some of the funds to buy something of better quality until the insurance check clears.

Paul watches us load it into the truck, his watery blue eyes almost gleeful, which is never a good sign. For how much bad blood is between Paul and I, this is going too easily. Maybe it's Lydia cooing over Jorge, asking if he's eating enough, if he's talked to his younger brothers lately, that is tempering the situation.

Personally, I find it hard to believe; Paul had no qualms about pointing a shotgun in my face the last time I was here, and Lydia was there for that, too!

Just like how Lydia stood by when Paul sold all of the inventory from the dealership, other than what was in Luck and their brothers' names, and she didn't say a thing when he pocketed the money. She was the named executor of Luck's parents estate, who was supposed to be the legal guardian of their younger brothers until they turned eighteen. Still, Luck dropped out of Julliard to raise their brothers, and Lydia let her husband bleed the estate dry all for the sake of keeping the peace. She may be sweet and caring, but I hold her equally responsible for Luck and Jorge's constant financial struggles.

However, Luck insists that family business should stay within the family. So I listen to them complain, give them advice they never take, and don't tell a soul what a piece of shit their uncle is.

Sure enough, just as I shut the tailgate and latch the back window of the topper, Paul clears his throat. "There's just the little matter of payment."

My fingers tighten around the handle of the topper window, and I take a breath to cool the spike of anger in my chest.

"Payment?" Rudy asks, his eyes wide as we exchange a glance.

Paul leans against the tailgate, forcing me to look at that smug smirk I would love to punch off his face. "Yes, payment. You boys got cash, or...?"

The silence lingers, as I struggle to figure out what to say.

Finally, Paul sneers. "You didn't come here thinking this would be free, did you?"

Burning with embarrassment, because yes, I'd assumed this junk would be free, I clear my throat. "Luck asked for a favor…"

"The favor is not calling the cops on you for daring to step foot on my property again, you hotheaded little shit!" Paul snaps, eyes narrowing for a moment before that smirk slinks back on his face. "But I suppose we can come to an agreement."

"Agreement?" Rudy asks. When he's on his back foot, he just repeats things like a parrot instead of arguing. It was easy to manipulate him as a kid. Now that he's twenty-five, he should really know better about controlling a conversation.

Paul waves a hand, that smug smile making my blood boil. "You boys seem to be in a bind, so I'll be reasonable. When do you think you'll be able to pay for all of this?"

I exchange a look with Jorge, whose fists are gripping the cuffs of his coat so tightly, his knuckles are white when he subtly leans into me. Fuck Paul Wilson. Jorge shouldn't have come. I take Jorge's hand, though it's probably not enough comfort with my thick gloves; this is too much stress for him. "Two weeks."

"Two weeks?" Paul grumbles. "Fine, whatever, two weeks then, and five hundred due. Sounds fair to me!"

"Five hundred bucks?!" I explode, "Are you fucking kidding? For this cheap ass shit? That would be a fraction of that at the hardware store!"

"Then why aren't you at the hardware store?" When I freeze, Paul laughs dryly. "That's what I thought. Just like your old man, both of you. Always broke and begging for scraps."

My mouth goes dry, and I mutter, "Better broke than a thief."

Paul takes one threatening step toward me. "The hell did you say to me?"

Despite Luck's voice in my head, asking me to calm down, to keep their family drama private, I raise my chin. "My dad may be shit with money, but he'd never steal from family." I choose to ignore all the wage theft; if Dad's business goes under, it falls on me to support the whole family, and I'd rather not shoulder that burden.

"Steal?!" Paul scoffs. "After all I did for those brats? Please, I should have taken more than a few measly cars!" He pauses, that glint back in his eye as he smirks. "Hell, maybe I *should* take more! Let's throw in the mutt, too! Who bought her? Me! Paid all that money for a useless pet! Might as well get a hunting dog out of the deal."

I step in front of Jorge, tightening my grip on his hand so he knows I still have him. "The *estate* paid for Olive! It was never your money!"

When I glance back at him, Jorge simply stands there, frozen and pale.

Bright red and fuming behind him, the rage on Rudy's face surprises me. I didn't know his class clown ass possessed a temper. He sneers, "If you lay a finger on Olive—"

"No one is taking the dog, mi cielo!" Lydia finally speaks up, pulling the stiff Jorge into a hug. His hand slips from mine, and I fight the urge to take my most sensitive friend back from the aunt who claims to love him, but never protects him. "I don't want a dog in my house! Okay? Olive isn't going anywhere!" She glares at me. "Let's move on from all this unpleasant talk! No one needs to hear about our family drama on the front lawn!"

I keep my angry retort of *"Maybe they do!"* to myself. Despite what Luck thinks, no one in this town would give Paul the time of day if they knew how he really treated the Alvarez family. But Luck loves their titi, and for their sake, I will keep my mouth shut.

"What if we return it?" Rudy blurts out. "Can we get this stuff back to you, in two weeks?"

I glare at him, confused. "Give it back? What, after the show, we open up the hole in the roof again?" But honestly, if it means not paying half a grand for shitty materials, I'll agree to anything.

"I'd rather have the money," Paul shrugs. "But sure, so long as everything—and I mean *everything!*—is back in my shed in two weeks time." Before I can agree to that bullshit, just so we can get out of here, he adds, "Then there's the small matter of collateral."

"Paul, really?" Lydia tsks.

"I just need to make sure they're good for it! This is my property they're borrowing, after all." Paul holds out his hands. "Let's say two weeks pass, and they don't have the money, what am I supposed to do? This is my capital I could be using."

"What the hell do you want, Wilson?" I ask.

"I think an agreement for something of equal value," Paul casually waves a hand, as if considering it. His movements are forced enough that I can tell he's been waiting for this opportunity. "Perhaps the Firebird, for example."

"Are you out of your mind?" I shout. "A mint condition collectible as collateral for rusty corrugated tin and some warped two-by-fours?"

Paul smirks, and my heart sinks; I've fucked up with my big mouth. "Well, if the condition is the quibble, then perhaps the Eldorado. It doesn't even have an engine."

"No!" I shake my head. "You're not taking Luck's—"

"Fine!" Jorge yells, his voice cracking. "If we don't have the supplies back to you in two weeks, we pay five hundred. And if we're not good for it, the Eldorado is yours."

I whirl around, disbelief that he's agreeing to this bullshit. "Jorge, that's not your call! That's Luck's car!"

"You're good for it, right, Felix?" Jorge interrupts me again, his jaw tight. His normally warm brown skin is so pale, he might pass out if I don't get him out of here soon. "With the fundraiser, and the show, and everything? You know Luck would rather lose the car than have the theater close, and *I* know you won't let them down."

I take one breath, two. Because I would rather cut off my right arm than let Luck down. "There's gotta be another way."

"But there isn't, is there?" Jorge shakes his head, stepping in closer to me to grip my shoulders. His hands shake through my coat. He whispers in my ear, "I sure as shit ain't got the money. Anything Luck has goes to Luis and Efrain's tuition. This is our only option. We just have to trust Sleighbell Springs will come through."

I glance up at his brown eyes, wide and trusting, so much like Luck's. "If we fuck this up, Luck is going to kill us."

Jorge's jaw tightens. "So we don't fuck it up, then."

Seven

Luck

"Arriba, abajo, al centro, y pa' dentro!" Six shot glasses smack on the table before I tilt the smooth tequila down my throat. Jorge and I exchange a smirk as Estelle grimaces, and Nome chokes. Hiding a wince, Aaron quickly bites into his lime. Like Jorge and I, Junie didn't bother with the salt and lime. Instead, she whoops like the party girl she is, ready for another round.

I slide Rudy's abandoned shot over to her; he quietly disappeared when Junie appeared with the tray during intermission. I can only assume he left to dance with Evalyn and Liam (both teachers at Dasher's and Prancer's), Twyla and Nisha, and a few of the burlesque students who wanted to celebrate the day-after-my-birthday at Sleigh Queen. While not quite as busy as during the tourist season, the gay bar still pulls in a crowd to watch the drag show and dance. The music thumps around our table, and I can just make out Rudy's fiery hair in the middle of the dance floor next to Keiran.

Neither Kelly brother likes to make it a big deal that they don't drink, so Rudy's sudden urge to dance was probably no coincidence. He would appreciate it if the shot happened to quietly disappear by the time he got back.

Junie happily obliges, tossing the silver liquor back like it's water, shimmying to the thumping beat of the music filling the bar. Her ample chest bounces in time, bumping against Jorge's crossed arms, who is wedged between her and Estelle in the VIP booth. He's sitting back as far as he can, arms tight around himself to avoid touching either of them. But his eyes still dart between Junie's cleavage, and the bare skin of Estelle's slender back, whenever she leans forward to talk to Aaron and Nome.

My brother's dating life (if he has one beyond pining for Felix) is a complete mystery to me, just as my nonexistent one is to him. Seeing him so off-balance by these two goddesses surrounding him is highly entertaining. He is such a recluse, I didn't expect him to actually come, but I'm glad he did. Jorge deserves to have fun. And despite his uncomfortable body language, he does seem to be having a good time.

"Listen up, my little gumdrops! We are back and ready to blow your back out!" May North sashays into the stage, her wig as big and bold as ever. "Who is ready for the second half of the show?"

I smile, swaying back and forth in my seat as the crowd cheers. That shot was only my third drink, but I love tequila. The warmth buzzes through me.

"I said! Who's ready for the second half of the show?!" May calls again.

I cheer along with the audience this time, pounding on the table.

"That's more like it!" May twirls and poses when she sees someone taking a picture of her. "Keep that same energy for our next performer! He's been bending over for you all night—"

"Oh my god, it's Felix!" I squeal.

Aaron is nice enough to squeal with me, but the rest of the table simply laughs at my excitement.

"Please welcome to the stage, the Short King of Sleigh Queen, Felix Navidad!"

Our table out-cheers the rest of the audience as a guitar riff plays. Felix struts onto the stage, his hips rolling in time with his shoulders in tight leather pants, combat boots, and a ripped fishnet shirt. His eyes are lined with thick, messy eyeliner, and his mullet is gelled as high as his curls can go. He smirks as he lip-syncs the My Chemical Romance song that the audience is screaming along to, breaking into cheers every time he pulls them in with his impressive athleticism or cocky swagger.

I need to focus. This is why I'm here tonight. Yes, it's the day after my birthday, but more importantly: I need to study Felix. Figure out why he can wrap this audience around his little finger with a dance that isn't particularly challenging or sexy, when we're still struggling hard when we rehearse our burlesque number.

My face falls. We're so stiff and awkward together, in a way we never used to be.

But here, on this stage, Felix simply extends a hand in a way that rolls through his body, and Aaron audibly groans out loud. That might be normal for Aaron, but even *I* felt that body roll in my soul. There's something...freer about him here.

"Why is he so hot?" I ask.

My friends burst into laughter. Even Jorge cracks a smile.

"No, I'm serious! What is he doing here that he's not doing in class?" I ask, unable to tear my eyes away from Felix's muscular thighs in those tight leather pants. He bends his knees into a deep squat that should look awkward. However, he manages to turn into something so sinful, that heat rushes through my whole body.

"He's performing?" Estelle suggests. "Instead of rehearsing? I know I always turn it out more with an audience."

"Jorge, what do you see?" I ask, finally tearing my eyes away when Felix starts crawling—luckily, crawling *away* from me, because there is no way in hell I'd be able to pull away from his blue eyes when I'm in his line of sight. His ass is fucking luscious and so incredibly biteable, but his eyes...I blink. Focus. I look at my brother, who I'm surprised to find smirking at me, instead of staring at *that* ass in *those* pants. "How does it feel, to see Felix dancing like this?"

"Really fucking weird, honestly." Jorge gives me a confused look. "He's my bro, you know? I don't want to see him shaking his ass like this."

"What?" I frown.

"Yeah, I kinda want to throw up in my mouth a little. No wonder Rudy left before his number." Jorge raises an eyebrow, and it almost looks like he's smirking at me. "Why, what do *you* see?"

"I don't know! Why would I know?" I laugh, too casually, too forced. Maybe Jorge doesn't want to admit his long-standing crush on Felix in front of everyone else? This town can be really nosy. "Nome, what do you think?"

Nome smirks. "I notice that he's alone, instead of with a partner."

"You think he doesn't want to dance with me?" I ask, heart sinking.

"No, not that! I think he wants to do way more than dance with you!" Nome teases. Junie and Estelle giggle. "I think he's finding it incredibly difficult to *only* dance with you! He's holding back with you in class, because he's trying way too hard to be respectful."

"I don't understand." My head spins. Was that a double shot of tequila?

"He's saying you need to fuck it out, babe!" Aaron says, before whistling at Felix; his leather pants are straining around his theatrically large packer as he lip-syncs in handstand splits.

"Nope!" I shake my head, panicking at the turn this conversation has taken. Especially in front of Jorge! "No, no, no! We do not!"

"Yes, yes, yes, darling!" Junie pats my arm sympathetically. "That man is down bad for you. Everyone in town knows it."

"No!" In a panic, I look at Jorge, who is covering his face with both hands, his shoulders shaking. Oh my god, is he crying? Is this conversation alone already breaking his sensitive heart? "But, no! He doesn't! Not at all! Jorge!"

"Hermane!" He pulls his hands away; laughter creases his face instead of tears. "You're so fucking clueless! You got that man whipped, dude. Are you serious? You had no idea?"

Nothing makes sense.

Jorge has been pining for Felix for fifteen years.

I frown. Hasn't he? He used to clam up and hug himself anytime Felix was around. Until they became closer, when I left for school, and I figured he'd finally learned to relax around his crush. Or...until Felix transitioned.

Clam up and hug himself. Just like he's doing now, with Estelle and Junie.

My jaw drops.

Oh my god. Is my brother straight?!

I look back to the stage, where Felix is collecting dollar bills from the audience as his number winds down, kissing the back of someone else's hand. He gives the woman a wink that makes my chest burn with jealousy.

It can't be my fault that we're so awkward together.

Can it?

Either my presence makes him unsure of what he's allowed to do, or I am so turned on anytime we dance together that I trip over my own feet. Maybe it's both.

Maybe Aaron's right. If Jorge and Felix are just friends, and he's not as off-limits as I've thought all these years... Maybe we do need to fuck it out.

I look at the empty shot glass clenched in my fist.

Maybe I've had too much tequila.

"Give it up for Felix Navidad, everyone!" May North saunters back onstage with a tray of shots balanced in the hand not holding the mic. "The ass full of sass, he's our beloved bendover boy here at Sleigh Queen! Felix, hunny, take this from me!"

Stuffing his tips into his waistband, Felix grabs the tray of shots from May. The wad of cash hides the crease of his hip, and I've never hated money more.

"Who do we have celebrating tonight?" May asks into the mic. "Any new jobs, bachelorettes, anniversaries, divorces, or birthdays?"

My friends cheer and shout, "It's Luck's thirtieth birthday!"

"It's the day after my birthday! My birthday was yesterday!" I protest.

Just my luck, my birthday fell on Friday the Day-Before-The-Fourteenth this year. Like every year, I opted to celebrate on the fourteenth, just to be safe. Already born on an unlucky number, I had the double misfortune to be born on a Tuesday. And for Puerto Ricans, at least according to Titi Lydia, Tuesday the Day-Before-The-Fourteenth is just as bad as a Friday. I was born with the odds stacked against me.

I thought I had beaten the mal de ojo that Titi Lydia always warned me about, growing up so happy and loved and full of dreams. Dreams that were so close to coming true, I could almost touch them, when it was all snatched away from me.

"Luck Alvarez! Get your ass onstage!" May calls me up, working the crowd for anyone else celebrating anything tonight.

Standing between a soon-to-be bride and a married gay couple celebrating an anniversary, I wait as May works down the line, asking each one questions about what they're celebrating. Felix hands each one a shot with strict instructions not to take it until May says.

After congratulating the married couple on five years together, she reaches me. May asks, "Felix, how many shots do we have left?"

"Four," he answers.

"Luck, babe, we're coming back to you." May skips me and moves to the bride-to-be, asking her about her upcoming nuptials. "Everyone, say it with me: Congratu-fucking-lations!"

The crowd cheers along, shouting "Congratu-fucking-lations!"

Everyone else does their shots, while I wait next to Felix, unsure of what's happening. Maybe I should come to Sleigh Queen more, so I'd know what was going on.

Once everyone else has left the stage, May turns to me. "Now, Mx. Luck! You turned the big Three-Oh yesterday! And we have exactly three shots left for you! Get on your knees, hunny!"

I glance at Felix, who nods.

Hesitantly, I kneel on the stage. This close up, Felix's mesh shirt clings to every muscle, riding up above his belly button. The bulge of his packer in his leather pants and that fucking hip crease end up right at eye level.

"One shot for every decade!" May calls, pulling my gaze back to her. "Everyone, count along with me!" I reach for the glass Felix holds out, but May smacks my hand away. "Just open wide, babe!"

With one more encouraging nod from Felix, I part my lips with a nervous smile, looking up at Felix, trusting he won't let me embarrass myself. His blue eyes smile down at me as he brings the glass to my lips.

"One!" May calls along with the crowd.

Felix tips the clear liquid into my mouth.

I swallow it easily. Too easily for well liquor, or even top-shelf.

He holds the next one up, smirking.

"Two!"

I drink it greedily, tongue darting out to wet my lips as I confirm my suspicions. The stage is hard under my knees, but I don't dare move, keeping my hands behind my back. "Felix, this—"

"Shh," he warns me quietly, bringing the third shot to my lips. "I know. But no one else needs to."

"Three!"

Eyes still caught by Felix's, I open my throat for the third shot of water. Because of course it's water. It may only be a shot, but I should have known Sleigh Queen would try to keep their patrons hydrated, instead of intoxicated.

Felix nods approvingly at me as he pulls me to my feet, his hand strong in mine.

As soon as we're at eye level again, the tension that's been plaguing me for the past two weeks is back. A hyperawareness of each other, a respectful distance we've both been keeping since that night our senior year of high school. A flood of desire fills me as his hand lingers to help me off the stage, the way it always anytime Felix does anything.

But this time, it's less terrifying.

I don't want to run anymore. I don't *have* to run anymore. Now, I want to analyze it, study it, figure out how we might use this tension to our advantage.

At least for the burlesque performance.

If Jorge *hasn't* been harboring a crush in Felix for years, I need to think about what that means. For Felix, for our friendship, for all of us. Tomorrow, anyway. And perhaps after I've had a chance to talk to Jorge in private, to make sure he was serious. Three shots of water isn't sobering enough to think clearly tonight, let alone have a heart-to-heart with my brother.

Tonight is for dancing.

Eight

Felix

Leather pants were a mistake.

I should have changed into shorts after the show. Dancing on the stage, this time as a go-go dancer to keep the crowd lively until bar close, always gets hot, even in the depths of winter. With a second layer of skin trapping my sweat, from gyrating hips to combat boot-clad toes, everything feels swampy.

But then I catch Luck looking from across the crowded dance floor. Their brown eyes drink in the sight of me, narrowing as their gaze travels from my chest to my hips. Their full, glossy lips close around the straw of their ice water. Despite their greedy gulps, a sheen of sweat covers their chest and forehead. The tip of their nose is red from how flushed they are.

Leather pants were the best idea I've ever had.

Perhaps Luck is just overheated, or tipsy. But that hazy expression is not their usual tell of being drunk. That's the face they've worn during our dance practices the past couple of weeks, the one that makes me hope that my feelings aren't one-sided. Either way, if I have Luck's attention, I want to keep it.

I dance harder, puffing out my chest to emphasize how broad my shoulders have grown. The red hair that coats my chest and stomach, and the leather band of the harness that cuts across my pecs. Testosterone, construction, and dancing here have finally given me muscles and a figure I love to show off.

Sweat makes the curls of my mullet cling to my neck, leaving my mustache damp and salty with each bead that drips down my face. After a week of working on the theater in between my usual gigs with Dad, and dancing with Luck after their classes are done for the day, every muscle in my body aches. I relish in the dull twinge of my thighs, my shoulders, the glorious burn that leaves me proud of the body grinding and shaking to the throbbing bass of the house music thumping through the crowd.

"Felix!" Luck calls. They must have left their friends and made their way through the crowd, because they're smiling up at me from next to the stage. They look up at me, a dreamy grin on their face and a glorious view down their skintight bralette, dampened with sweat so every luscious curve is exposed to view; taut nipples strain against the thin pink lace.

Normally, I'd look away. But normally, we'd be in public, in view of people I don't necessarily want to see me so closely. We'd be in front of their dance class, or our brothers, or this town that can't mind its own business. However, Jorge left after the show, and Rudy disappeared somewhere. With their departure, there's no one watching who would tease me tomorrow. Besides Aaron, and all my coworkers, but they'll tease me either way.

Sleigh Queen gets a different version of me than the rest of this town. This place is where I can be free and let loose, and everyone in town lets me get away with being a bit more...cocky than I normally would be.

So I look back at Luck as much as they've been looking at me tonight, how they've been looking at me the past couple weeks of dance rehearsal. It's a relief, to take my fill of the dusting of freckles along their collarbone, the miles of light brown skin exposed by their barely-there top, after the jacket they came with was discarded early on.

Luck is flushed when I finally drag my eyes up their neck, the tip of their nose red again. "Felix!" they shout again, their smile more dazed than goofy now.

I bend into a squat to hear them better, preening as their eyes dart to the packer bulging between my parted thighs. "What's up?"

Dragging their eyes from my crotch, they look up at me with a pout. "We gotta figure this out."

"Figure what out?" For some reason, their question brings out a curl of nerves in my chest. Whether it's anxiety or anticipation, I'm not sure.

"Why you're different!" Luck calls. "Why we don't dance together like we used to!"

"I transitioned!" I tease. "So did you!"

"Yeah, but we're still us!" they insist. "You were Felix before you transitioned, and I don't dance any differently than I used to!"

I laugh. "Yes, you do!"

"How?" they ask with a scoff.

"How am *I* different?" I return, stealing the water from their hand to take a sip. I sit on the stage so we can talk more easily over the music. "Who I am deep down hasn't changed—much—but I let the real me out more now. Especially here. You do, too. Remember when you were the Sugarplum Fairy when you were in high school, and how different it was when you danced that role again after college?"

"Yeah, I realized I wasn't a good fit for that part." Luck wrinkles their nose. "Estelle is way better at it than I ever was!"

"My point is: it was the same dance, the same routine, but how you performed it completely changed." I hold out a hand to them. "I'll show you."

After a moment of trepidation, Luck takes my hand. I pull them up with me as I stand, gloating at their thrilled giggle as I easily haul them onto the stage. With the chairs and tables stacked up here to make room for the dance floor, there's just enough room for one person to dance comfortably.

With two, we're pressed chest to chest.

"Imagine you don't know you're genderqueer yet. Imagine I'm someone else," I say in their ear, to make sure they can hear me over the music. My hand slips around their waist, hovering over the bare skin of their back. Am I allowed to touch them right now? "Pretend you're Lucia and only Lucia, not Luck, and you're hitting it off with some guy at a bar you've never met before. How would you dance?"

Luck immediately turns around, grinding into me with the bountiful ass that haunts my dreams. My packer presses against my dick under my jockstrap. Fighting a whimper, I bite my lip. They lean back, arms around my neck. Their lips tease my ear as they say, "You should grab my hips."

"Oh, should I?" I tease, hesitating only a moment before sliding my hands along Luck's bare skin, barely biting back a groan at how fucking soft and warm the skin of their waist is under my hands. Just like I have every time we've rehearsed the number that is slowly pulling me apart with every rehearsal.

This is exactly what I expected from Lucia Alvarez: grinding on me like a seductress the second they sense what I want from them. Back then, we were both fulfilling the roles we were playing. The performance came easily, like second nature, because we'd been taught the rules that never fit us our whole lives.

Luck is still Lucia in many ways; probably why they don't feel pulled to change their name. Why they're comfortable with both feminine pronouns and gender-neutral ones, without a hint of wrongness. Why they feel so at ease emphasizing the lushness and curves of their body against mine, each slow roll of their hips tantalizing.

They're still Lucia, right alongside Luck. Unlike me, their femininity is not a pained performance. When they want to be, Luck can be incredibly seductive. They simply downplay their power, for some reason I don't understand.

Luck's friends must finally notice us dancing together, because Aaron's scream cuts across the bar.

My quiet laugh makes a few tendrils of Luck's hair escape their bun. "Now, you're you. All Luck, the person you are now. And I'm whoever you want me to be." God, isn't that the truth? "How would you dance with me now?"

Luck spins in my arms, their face oh so close to mine. They roll their eyes. "You made your point."

Fuck my point. I want to dance with Luck. *Really* dance with Luck. Not perform for others. Just Luck and me, our bodies moving with the music, together. I shake my head. "How would Luck dance with a stranger now?"

They raise an eyebrow, brown eyes digging into me. "You're no stranger. You're Felix."

My breath catches in my throat. "Even better. Show me."

"Fine!" Luck huffs. Their hands find my hips and tug me close. I fight to keep from melting at the strong grip at my waistband. When one hand slides around to the small of my back, I fail utterly, fusing my body against theirs. Their other hand slips up my bare stomach and chest, palm sliding easily against my slick skin.

Oh god, what if I stink? "Sorry, I'm sweaty—"

"Shut up. You're so..." Luck interrupts, their eyes flicking up to mine as they wedge a thigh in between mine. "God, Felix, you have no idea!"

Each inhale is an uphill battle as my chest tightens and desire burns through me. At half-tempo to the house music playing, Luck rolls their hips side to side, oh so slow, dragging me along with them in an intimate bachata. Their featherlight touch is all the command I need to twist in sync with them.

Luck's hand climbs up my chest, my neck, fingers burying into my sweat-soaked hair. They yank my head back, exposing my throat to them, and I can't help but moan, knees trembling to keep myself upright.

Helpless in their grip, Luck spins me so my back is to their chest. Hand hard around my hip, they murmur in my ear, "Take the tip."

"What?" I sputter, confused. I'll take anything Luck wants me to, in *all* of my holes, but what tip am I taking?

Luck laughs quietly in my ear. "You have fans waiting to tip you, cariño. Take the tips." Hand still wrapped in my curls, they push me forward, bending me in half to face a cluster of dollar bills being shoved in my face.

Awareness of where we are, who is around us, snaps me back to reality. Around the platform, a crowd of the regulars at Sleigh Queen are gloating at me. I'm bent over with my ass pressed against Luck's hips, their hand letting go of my hair to pull my harness tight around my chest, tugging me where they want me.

Strangely, I am not embarrassed in the least, other than that I forgot anyone would witness this unforgettable moment. No, this is exactly where I want to be at all times. What would I possibly have to be ashamed of? Everyone here knows how I feel about them, and is familiar with my submissive and exhibitionist tendencies. I am proud to be bent over for Luck, in front of everyone. This is vindication really, for all the years I've dreamt of this, for all the times people told me to move on from them. For all the people who have tried and failed to measure up in Luck's place.

"Go on, cariño." Luck pushes me towards the edge of the stage to collect my—our—earnings. "Take it."

Shit-eating grins on their faces, Junie and Aaron are among the waiting patrons, waving a wad of singles in each hand.

"If you say a goddamn word about this," I warn Aaron as I tug the cash out of his hand. Fat good it will do; out of all of my friends, Aaron gives me the most shit. His gossipy ass works as a barista at the Brew House, so everyone in Sleighbell Springs will hear about this within days.

"You have no power over me." Aaron kisses my cheek with a wink. "I will never shut up about this!"

When my hands are full of bills and only teasing looks remain, Luck pulls me back up, their grip on my harness stronger than I expected. "Aaron thinks we should fuck it out."

"What?" I whimper, leaning my head back on their shoulder as I sag in Luck's arms. There is no possible way the words I just heard were what Luck really said!

"Aaron thinks we should fuck it out," Luck repeats, slower and clearer and directly in my ear. As if I didn't hear them the first time. "He thinks we have too much sexual tension getting in our way."

"How much have you had to drink?" I ask, my mouth going dry. Did that sound like a proposition? I can't tell if I meant it that way or not. But if Luck wants to take it that way...

Luck freezes. "I'm not *that* drunk, Felix. I know it's a bad idea." They pause before their voice softens with hurt. "I just thought you'd find it funny."

Oh, Luck did not take my question as a proposition at all. My stomach sinks. "Luck, I didn't mean—"

"I know what you meant, Felix," they snap, pulling away. Before I can stop them, Luck hops off the stage.

My sweat-soaked back is chilled without them pressed against it. I stare helplessly at Luck's retreating form, pushing through the crowd towards the bathrooms. "Aaron! Take over for me!"

"Oh my god, yes! I get to practice my sexy dances on a stage!" Aaron hops onto the platform, pulling off his shirt without prompting. "Go after your not-a-girl, Felix!"

I'm already halfway through the crowd, shoving the bills in my hands into the waistband of my jockstrap, because these damn pants don't have pockets. Anticipation burns through me.

For twelve years, Luck has kept me at arm's length, pushing me away any time I've tried to talk about that night our senior year, the night we kissed. Eventually, I gave up. Tried and failed to move on from the claim they've laid on my heart since we were teenagers. So why, after twelve years, would Luck take that personally? Why would they act like I'd rejected them, if they didn't want...

"Luck!" I catch up to them before they reach the restroom, pulling them by the elbow into the supply closet. "What was that?" Crossing their arms with a huff, Luck avoids my eyes as I close the door behind us. The music is muted here. All I can hear is my pulse roaring, and Luck's shallow breaths. "What was that?" I ask again, not bothering to turn the light on. The faint illumination from the exit sign is enough to see by.

"It was just an idea," they mutter, curling around themself.

"Do you want that?" My voice trembles with hope, with dread. "To 'fuck it out'?"

Luck shrugs one shoulder. "It's not the worst idea."

It is. The worst idea.

Because on no plane of any earthly existence would anything between Luck and I be mere fucking. Even without the undying adoration that I've been carrying for them for years, we have decades of friendship, of history, of connection that no one but each other quite understands. One kiss all those years ago almost broke us.

They glance past me, avoiding my eyes. "Do you?"

"Do I what?" I ask. "Want to fuck it out?"

They nod, staring at the floor, though the closet is so cluttered we barely have an inch between us.

"Luck..." I sigh, hating how they refuse to look at me. Because how have they not seen it? All these years, how could they miss the love in every fiber of my existence, whenever I've looked at them? My hand reaches out on its own accord, tilting their chin up until those brown eyes finally meet mine.

Luck holds my gaze, a stubborn set to their quivering chin, as if they're afraid I'm about to reject them.

I exhale in a soft sigh, "Fuck it," and lean in.

The kiss was supposed to be soft, tentative. I meant to give Luck time to pull away before my lips touched theirs, in case they didn't want it.

But Luck meets me halfway, already reaching for me, hand twining through the hair at the back of my neck to pull me closer.

Our lips crash together, hard and needy and demanding.

As always, I melt under their touch, sinking into every point of contact, in hopes of being consumed. My arms wrap around their waist, pulling them tight enough to dip them back, turning us to press them against the door.

When my tongue parts their lips, Luck moans, and oh, it takes everything in me not to sink to my knees and bury my face between their legs to hear that sound again. Their body arches against mine, thick thigh hitching over my hip to grind against my packer, the pressure through my pants tantalizing against my dick. Their tongue laps inside my mouth, their hands exploring every inch they can reach.

I squeeze their ass, encouraging them to keep going, to give us more of the pleasure that feels so right after so many years of dreaming of this moment. To my delight, Luck fucking whimpers and rocks their hips against me. "Luck, can I touch you?"

Freezing in my arms, Luck tears their lips away from mine. "No!"

I stumble back as if they've slapped me. Tripping over the broom, I catch myself before I land ass-first into a mop bucket. "No?"

"No!" Luck shakes their head, pressing their fingers to their lips. Their eyes are wide, aghast as they stare at me. "We can't!"

"We can't?" I blink, confused. They were enjoying that, too. Right? "Why?"

"Because!" Luck blinks rapidly, and panic seizes my chest. Have I misread the signals that badly? I never meant to scare them, to hurt them. They don't seem drunk, but maybe they've had more than I thought? They gasp, their voice pitching higher. "Because! We can't! Tonight is for dancing!"

"Okay." I hold out my hands palm out, moving them in time with my steadying breaths, the way I do for Jorge's panic attacks. Thankfully, Luck breathes with me automatically, their gasps slowing as they match my inhale. "Okay, we can't, so we won't. Are you okay?"

"Yes! I'm sorry! I shouldn't have done that!" Luck shakes their head. "I just...I am so confused."

Relief fills me, and I have to fight a laugh. They did want that. They just think they shouldn't. Typical Luck. Just like that night, all those years ago. "Why shouldn't we?"

They never answered the question then, and I don't expect them to now.

As predicted, they shake their head. "You're going to laugh at me if I tell you."

"I won't."

"Oh, you will!" Luck's snort is sardonic. "I'm laughing at myself, but I'm still so- I'm so...confused. And I need some time. To think."

"Okay." I nod, pulling them into a hug, already missing the charged intimacy between us. It's a weight off my chest when they hug me back. "Are you okay? I'm sorry, I just thought you wanted—"

"Don't apologize!" Luck laughs into the bare skin of my shoulder. "I did want. I do! I just don't know if fucking it out is actually a good idea. For us."

A pang of hurt strikes my chest, and my eyes burn. "Right." Was that all they wanted? To fuck it out? I pull away from our hug. Our sweat-damp skin pulls apart as I do, and every inch stings as much as my eyes. "We both need space to think. But dancing together tonight helped, right?"

"Right!" Luck smiles, too brightly. "We'll get this routine down in no time!"

Relieved it's dark enough that they won't see the red around my eyes, I smile back, opening the door so Luck can return to their friends. "Well, uh, happy birthday, Luck."

"It's the day after my birthday." Luck flushes, leaning into the shadow I'm hiding in to kiss my cheek as they pass. "But thanks, Felix."

I close the door behind them once they're gone, leaning against the cool metal. Running a hand along my face, I take a deep breath, and another, and another, until the threat of tears has passed.

Nine

Luck

"Luck, you okay locking up tonight?"

How dare he? I frown, jaw tightening as Felix hangs up his Backstreet Boys outfit, laughing with everyone in the greenroom of the Sleighbell Stage; Nome fell on xis ass trying to tear xis pants off during rehearsal, and Avery hasn't let xim forget it yet. As nice as it is to see Avery confident enough, *relaxed* enough, to tease the boy band's unofficial leader a mere week before our showcase, I am too furious to appreciate the moment.

How could I be anything but angry, when Felix is casually standing around in the spacious dressing room, in his tight shorts and nothing else? Every inch of pale, freckled skin is temptation incarnate, especially now that I know how it feels under my hands. How those muscles move against my belly and chest. How his pink lips with the ginger scruff feel when my tongue is down his throat. How dare he kiss me? He had no right to make me want him.

"Earth to Luck!" A hand waves in front of my face.

I jump, automatically smiling up at Twyla. "Oh! Hey!"

She raises an eyebrow and purses her lips. A flick of her eyes toward Felix and back brings my frown right back.

"Can I help you?" I ask impatiently. Between Jorge's smirks, Aaron and Junie's waggling eyebrows, and Estelle's knowing looks, I can't wait for the teasing to be over. At least no one seems to know about that glorious kiss, or that I was dry humping his packer in the supply closet. I squeeze my eyes shut as I pretend to scratch my forehead, trying not to think about how close I was to coming all over him from a few minutes of making out. Trying to get my thoughts in order so I can gather the courage to talk to Jorge with a cool head has been impossible.

Twyla looks tempted to keep teasing me, but thankfully she changes the subject. "You okay to lock up? You and Felix were planning on rehearsing more after class, right?"

"Oh, yeah!" I had said that. Yesterday. *Before* my day-after-my-birthday party took an unexpected and overwhelming turn. Felix and I still haven't talked about it. I don't know what to say to him either. But if Felix and I can't manage to simply practice a dance routine without the riot of my feelings getting in the way, we have much bigger problems. "That's still okay, right?"

"Yeah, of course!" Twyla nods. "Felix has a key, though, so he can work on the roof, and Nisha and I haven't had a date night in a while, so I was thinking..." She rubs her hands together eagerly, smirking like the charming stud she is. "I could take off a bit early and make her dinner? Beat this storm home that we're supposed to get tonight. If that's cool with you, of course."

"Oh! Oh course!" I gush. "Yes, go on your date night! Felix and I can lock up! No problem!"

Some problem, actually.

Many problem.

Big problem.

But my soul-crushing embarrassment that I misread Jorge and Felix's friendship so so *so* incorrectly, for so long, should not stop Twyla from giving her wife the princess treatment Nisha deserves.

Nor is this overwhelming need for Felix, that I've suppressed since I was a teenager until it exploded into an unleashable, raging storm last night, Twyla's problem. I just have to find a way to navigate it. The way one might find their way through a blizzard on foot, uphill, barefoot, in the dark.

"Cool!" Twyla looks almost embarrassed by her eagerness. "I got everything else shut down but the lights. So if you just hit the main switch in the booth, and the other one in the office before you go—I've got them both marked with a sticky note."

"Twyla, I've shut down the theater before." I snort. "I got it, don't worry. Go make dinner for your wifey."

Twyla presses her hands together, thanking me a few more times, before she runs away.

With a smile, I look at the class gathered around me. "Great job today, Sexy Santas! It felt different right, doing it onstage? More real?"

Heads nod among the group. For once, Felix doesn't catch my eye to quietly mock the class nickname. The corner of his lip twitches, but he stays looking at his feet as he leans against the wall. My chest twinges, but I keep my smile bright.

"The theater will be open for anyone who wants to rehearse more on Thursday, and we're meeting at four for a final dress rehearsal on Friday!" I beam. "I've sent you all the setlist, with our guest performers from Sleigh Queen and Jingle My Bells woven in there. If you have any questions, or need anything at all in the next week, email me. Text me. Send me a carrier pigeon." I beam at the group's reluctant snorts in response to my bad joke. "We will figure it out, and everything will be fine!"

Unless we don't raise enough money.

But that won't be their fault.

It will be mine, because this was all my idea.

I swallow the nagging feeling that I'm forgetting something, but I can't think of what it could be. "Be sure to remind all of your friends and family about it!" I add, just in case it makes a difference.

"Remember, they're here to celebrate your courage, and if they or you are not comfortable with them witnessing your courage firsthand, they can still make a donation to the fundraiser in your honor!"

The class nods and says their goodbyes, half looking excited at the prospect of our upcoming recital next weekend. The other half, Avery especially, looks downright terrified as they troop out the door.

Finally, it's only Felix and I in the greenroom.

"You can wear whatever you want," I blurt out, fiddling with the lace of the garter I'll be wearing during the second group number, which I rehearsed with the class earlier. "For the rehearsal, I mean. Tonight. I should change. The rainbow dress. It comes apart." I huff, annoyed at my awkwardness. "I mean, that's the point. But I should put it on. So you can take it off."

Felix presses his lips together, and nods, blue eyes amused at my nervous rambling. "I'll, uh, be onstage, then. Let you change."

"Okay," I whisper, as he lets himself out of the greenroom, kneepads in hand.

I stumble through the outfit change, though I'll have to be much faster during the show. There's plenty of time between "Titi Me Pregunto" and "Francesca," but I want to watch my students as much as I can. I leave the rainbow feathered Carnival headpiece on the counter, though I should practice dancing with it this week. I need to practice securing it first.

By the time I make my way out, Felix is bare chested, clad only in shorts, skin-toned kneepads, and his half-sole dance shoes. We never discussed footwear with our costumes, but we have both been rehearsing in lyricals. It feels right, somehow, to be nearly barefoot. A throwback to the modern classes we used to take together.

"Luck, you're..." Felix pauses as his eyes trace down my body. "You look great."

"Thanks." I smooth my corset, pressing down on the Velcro securing it to the skirt pieces swishing around my hips. "The sections are velcroed together, but take them off in ROY G BIV order, okay? Purple is the base layer, so if you pull that first, the whole thing is coming off at once."

Felix nods, eyes still drinking me in in a way that makes me fight to keep from posing for him. The way I did Saturday, when he told me to dance like Lucia would have.

It's not that Lucia isn't me anymore. I'm still me, always have been and always will be. But I have grown so much that Lucia isn't enough to contain all of me anymore. Lucia is merely the younger, innocent part of me that accepts what other people give—the side of me that bends over for people to make them happy. That's still me, and I love that generous, understanding, and naive part of me too. However, along the journey of understanding myself, I've learned that I also like to take, to demand, to direct the world around me.

But young Lucia hadn't learned that yet, hadn't learned what it meant to lose something. Young Lucia would never have clung to everything good for as long as possible, at any cost the way I do now. Young Lucia would never have been hesitant to ask for what she wanted, for fear of losing it.

In the silence of the stage, a gust of wind howls outside. The sound alone makes me shiver. In hindsight, maybe Jorge and Felix's imagined crush was to keep my own at bay. To keep myself safe from the risk of losing my best friend.

"Where do we start?" Felix asks quietly, pulling me from my thoughts. "Should we run through without music at first? Figure out what we're doing in this space, instead of the studio?"

I nod. "I'll, uh...be here. I'll be over at the pulley to secure the silks after the aerial number, and stay onstage, dancing by myself while you're still picking up the tips."

"Should I do a double take?" Felix smirks, turning around from his side of the stage to look at me over his shoulder. "While bending over?"

I snort, amused as always at how much this grumpy man loves to show his ass off. "Yeah, ham it up all you want. We're starting off cheesy and corny, remember?"

"Then what?" Felix asks, straightening. He turns on his heel, legs taking long, slow steps as he circles the stage toward me.

"Then the music changes, and you try to catch me." I shrug, spinning slowly on the ball of my foot. "And once you grab the end of the red section, I'll run."

Felix stalks toward me, knees bent as he pretends to hide, freestyling his pursuit with some floor work and spins. The second he reaches his hand out, I stop spinning, acting shocked to see him. I pause long enough to let him pinch the end of the red strip of fabric covering my right hip, then glissade away from him, before I jeté across the stage. The thin Velcro rips apart, and the top layer peels off, exactly how I designed it.

I face the imagined audience, acting hurt and embarrassed about the exposed section of my hip, until I pretend to realize how good it looks, and play up the new slit in my skirt. I bump my hip one, one-two, one-two-three times to the music in my head.

Only to feel Felix's tug on the orange silk, and the rush of air against my skin as it falls away from me. With an assemblé, I hop a small distance away. I don't know how he snuck up on me, but I trust Felix to tap into that cockiness he displayed onstage last night. To let that confidence that's been growing in him since he first came out as trans surface, instead of deferring to me, the way he has been in past rehearsals.

As we run through the routine we've put together in the last few weeks, we manage to tap into something. Not quite as in sync as we used to be, before we stepped into who we are now. But we find a balance. Each strip of fabric gives Felix more swagger and me more sensuality, until there's only the purple left. As we've rehearsed, he kneels and crawls to me, begging to touch the corner of the strip circling my wide hips. I pull him to his feet, tease him as we dance together, until I finally put the hem of the purple fabric in his hand.

Grabbing onto the waistband as he tugs, I let it send me twirling across the stage. I stop as soon as the fabric pulls taught between us. Felix reels me in, and I twirl back to him, wrapping the fabric around my waist and hips until he catches me in his arms. Blue eyes stare me down, burning with all the intensity and desire and adoration I imagined in the dark of the supply closet last night.

Frozen, I drink in Felix's parted lips and sweat-sheened skin. He's supposed to dip me. Why isn't he dipping me? Instead, his hands, rough and calloused, scrape up my hips oh so slowly.

"Luck," Felix breathes, squeezing the curves of my waist. He's supposed to be unlacing the gold corset. I should tug it off myself, get us back on track.

Instead, I cup his jaw. My thumb strokes his cheek, touching the corner of his lips. My gasp when Felix kisses the pad comes out in a shudder, drowned out by a crash and roar from above.

The lights dive into darkness, and the wind howls louder than ever.

I yelp when freezing rain spritzes my bare skin.

"Fuck!" Felix curses under his breath, pushing away from me. "That fucking useless ass rotten ass sheet metal!"

"Felix?" I call, unsteady on my feet without his arms supporting me. But he doesn't answer. There's only cold wind, icy rain pelting me, and darkness. My head spins, unable to see anything around me. What did I do this time? I've been so careful to not jinx myself—I forgot to knock on wood earlier! During my pep talk!

My chest tightens as a door bangs open, and stomping feet climb the catwalk steps.

Is he...heading to the roof? In the dark? And the icy sleet?

"No. No. He'll fall!" Blood roars in my ears as tears fill my eyes. "He's not even wearing shoes! At least my parents had shoes on! At least Jorge had a coat."

Falling to my knees, I curl around myself, helpless with fear. The rushing winter storm against my nearly naked body makes me shiver uncontrollably. In the dark, I can't see beyond my hands. Each breath is a struggle. Any shuddering inhale I manage in between sobs is not enough. My head spins, as if I might pass out.

I'm not sure how much time passes in the dark. Enough that the roar of the wind outside dulls, when the echoing clang of footsteps sounds on the catwalk steps again.

The sobs return to wrack my body, this time in relief.

"Luck?" Cold wet hands grasp my shoulders. "Are you okay?"

"You're alive!" I fall into Felix's arms. "You didn't fall!"

His skin is icy, clammy, the way Jorge's was in the hospital before he woke up. Countless hours in a snowstorm, unconscious on the side of the freeway with our parents' bodies, left him with hypothermia. By the time I got to the hospital, hours after he was found, my brother still felt like a corpse when I took his hand.

Fresh tears well in my eyes. They should have never visited me that weekend. I should never have invited them to my performance. Why had they come, when there was a snowstorm in the forecast?

Felix's skin warms under my touch as his arms clasp around me. "Deep breaths, Luck. You're safe. You're having a panic attack." He cradles the back of my head. "I'm sorry I left, I wasn't thinking. I just wanted to make sure the sheet metal didn't blow away." He presses his cheek to my hair, hand rubbing a slow path up and down my spine. "But it's okay. I nailed it all back down, and you're safe, and I'm safe, and the theater will be fine, and your car isn't going anywhere, and everything is okay. Okay?"

I nod into his shoulder, dampening his already-soaked skin with my tears. After a few deep breaths in time with his, inhaling the musky sweat and the cold rain soaked into his curls, I manage to ask, "Why would my car go anywhere?"

"Oh fuck me," Felix mutters, freezing. "Jorge didn't tell you?"

"Tell me what?" I ask. Dread fills me when I pull away. "Felix? What does the Eldorado have to do with anything?"

"Luck, this is not a good time to tell you about that," Felix murmurs, his voice too calm, too steady to be anything but placating. "Can I take you home and tell you there? I promise, I will tell you, but if you're gonna yell at me, you should yell at Jorge too."

Anger replaces the panic in my chest. "I don't like this, Felix."

"I know, Luck. And we should have told you weeks ago." Felix's hands find mine, and he pulls me to my feet. How he can see in the pitch-dark is beyond me, because I can barely make out his pale skin in the black. "But from what I saw from the roof, the power is out all over town, and I want to make sure you're somewhere safe and warm before I stress you out more."

He leads me to the greenroom. With our phones against the mirrors, he lights up the room enough to gather our belongings and pull warmer clothes on. I barely remember the light switches Twyla asked me to turn off. Felix disappears in a flash the second I mention them, returning in record time to guide me back through the wings to the door, where his pickup and Bertha are parked.

He loads Bertha into the bed of his truck, and for once I can't find it in myself to argue that I can bike home just fine.

I am a trembling mess, my head pounding. Biking right now would be utterly foolish.

Instead, I stare at the passenger door, willing myself to reach out and open the handle.

"Luck?" Felix touches my back. "You okay?"

"Yeah!" I chirp automatically. "Of course!"

Felix opens the door for me and waits patiently, despite the pelting, freezing rain.

"I..." I shake my head, frustration leaking out of my eyes, but my body isn't cooperating. "I can't get in."

"Okay. You don't have to." Softly, Felix shuts the door, locking it with a beep of his key fob. "We can go to my place. Bertha will be okay in the truck overnight. Just a few blocks to walk. Is that okay?"

At my nod, Felix takes my hand and leads me down Mistletoe Street. The normally festive main street being this dark and silent is eerie. Freezing rain mixes with the tears staining my cheeks, and I lean into Felix's side.

How dare he?

First he kisses me, opening the floodgates to all of the feelings I've tried to forget all these years. And now? Now, he reminds me why I fell in love with him in the first place. Why I'm still in love with him, after all these years.

Ten

FELIX

I︎F I HAD KNOWN that Luck would be spending the night with me, I would have taken the garbage out this morning. Or washed any dishes in the past two days. Or put the laundry away, instead of stacking it on the only comfortable seat in my cluttered studio apartment. Thank God the power is out. The dark hides all of my slothful habits.

Oh, I should change the sheets! When was the last time I did that?

Fortunately, Luck has known what a slob I can be since we were in elementary school. They are kind enough—or perhaps still locked in their head enough—to not say anything about any smells or clutter they might be running into as I hurry through the pitch-dark room to pick up the cleanish laundry from my clothes chair.

As if to mock me, the lights flick on and the appliances sputter back to their gentle hum. I clutch the pile of clean clothes to my chest, and gesture for Luck to sit.

They hover in the doorway, staring at their feet.

"Luck?" I ask, carefully so as not to push them. Like Jorge, Luck has always been anxious. Their bubbly personality makes it easy to forget, sometimes, just how bad it can be. How much worse it got after their parents passed. Luck works so hard to hide it, burying their pessimism beneath bright smiles and kind enthusiasm. Trying to get them to open up about it simply makes them double down on their cheer.

But I've never seen Luck have a panic attack until tonight.

Jorge, yes—less so now than when he first came home from the accident, now that he's had years to heal, now that he has Olive. He's said Luck gets them too, but they're always so careful to put on a brave face, even around me. That's just Luck's way. Hiding the pain and the fear and the doubt, because they're the oldest and they've always had to. Just like how they dropped out of Julliard after the accident, so Jorge, Efrain, and Luis wouldn't have to move in with Paul and Lydia.

"Luck," I say, a little more firmly. "Come sit down."

"Oh!" They jump, hugging themself. "Oh, I'm okay!"

With a huff, I shake my head, and drop my clean laundry into the dirty laundry pile on the floor. Probably all needs washing again anyway. Hands around their shoulders, I steer them to the chair. "That wasn't a question. Sit."

"My boots are still on." Luck sits when I push them into the chair, pursing their lips in annoyance, because I won't let them be a martyr if they don't have to be. How rude of me.

"Do you want a shower?" I ask, kneeling down to pull their boots off, so they don't talk themself into walking home. "I have some clothes you can sleep in. Or if you want to sit quietly for a while, I can make you some tea first."

"I should shower," Luck nods. But they make no move to get up. I fill the tea kettle I never use with water, and find some chamomile tea in the back of the cabinet. Luck seems to think I'm a fan of herbal tea, like they are; they gave me both the kettle and the tea as a Christmas present a few years ago. The only tea I drink is what Luck makes for me.

Luck is staring at the laundry pile when I bring them the mug, and they jump when I hold it out to them. "Oh, Felix, you didn't have to—"

"Just take it," I interrupt, already impatient with their insistence that no one ever do anything nice for them.

They huff, but take the mug from me.

"Thank you."

"That's my line," Luck teases, cradling the steaming mug to their chest. Their eyes return to the pile of laundry, unfocused.

Concern makes my stomach tense, but I force myself to give Luck space. They'll talk when they're ready. At least they won't notice me changing the sheets—they'd want to help.

I get as far as tucking in the top sheet when a pillow buffets my head.

"Felix! How dare you?" Luck growls.

"What did I do?" I roll my eyes, yanking the pillow from their hands. Of course, Luck put the pillowcase on before smacking the shit out of me with it.

"I would have helped!" Luck crosses their arms. "I've just been sitting here being a sad bitch, and you've been changing the sheets?! For me?"

"Well, more for my pride," I mutter, grabbing the other pillowcase before they can take it. "While this is a very gender-affirming reminder that I am just a man, I don't want to be *that* much like a cis man. I do change my sheets...sometimes."

Luck snorts, reaching for the other pillow. "You're ridiculous."

I snatch it out of their hands. "And *you're* not going to make my bed for me. I am hosting you tonight, I can clean up after myself a little bit."

"Your mess never bothered you when we were kids," Luck snarks.

"Because we were kids," I mutter, burning in embarrassment. Between my mom's chronic fatigue and my dad's drinking, a certain level of mess was normal in our house. Everything I know about keeping a home, I learned from the Alvarezes, and did my best to teach Rudy. "I didn't know any better yet."

"Okay, fine, but you should know by now that I don't care about how clean your place is!" Luck hugs themself again, face falling. "You're being too sweet."

"You think this is sweet?" I scoff, shaking the comforter out before draping it over the bed. "We've been friends since we were five, Luck. Inviting you to sleep in my messy, tiny apartment when the weather is shit is the bare minimum." As I tuck in the corners, I take a deep breath to gather my courage, because I owe Luck an explanation now that the worst of their panic attack seems to have passed. Something I should have told them weeks ago, something I'd assumed their brother would, something I had hoped they would simply never find out about because I wasn't going to let them down. "Do you want to shower first, or should I tell you something you should actually be mad about?"

Luck frowns, their eyes narrowing. "Tell me, and I'll process in the shower before yelling at you."

My sigh comes out more like a hiss. "Paul's favor had some conditions."

"Of course," Luck tsks.

"I should have told you sooner, but I was hoping Jorge would, or that I'd come up with some money from somewhere, so we didn't have to worry about it, but..." I wince, hating the weak excuses leaving my mouth instead of the truth. "Basically, if we don't have the supplies back to Paul the day after the showcase, we pay five hundred." Sitting on the end of the bed, I hesitate, then add, "And if we're not good for it, the Eldorado is his."

"What?" Luck cries. "Felix, that's not yours to give!"

"I know." I stare at the clothes rumpled on the floor. "He insisted on collateral. It was your car or Jorge's, and..."

"Was Jorge there?" Luck asks quietly. "He knew about this, agreed to it?"

I nod, still staring at the laundry pile.

The silence drags on longer than I expect. I almost want Luck to yell at me for agreeing to this bullshit in the first place, for not telling them for so long. I should have known better than to deal with Paul. I should have tried harder to find something else, or asked to borrow money from May or something.

But Luck simply plucks a towel, washcloth, T-shirt, and boxers from the clean clothes at the top of the laundry pile, and disappears into the bathroom.

With a sigh, I start folding the clothes that have been living in rumpled piles for months, to kill time until the inevitable come-to-Jesus from Luck. They usually take really long showers, and I'm sure they'll use all the hot water. My tiny apartment doesn't have the fancy water heater I installed for them years ago. By the time Luck reappears from the bathroom, I've got most of the clean clothes folded neatly on the foot of the bed, and the dirty clothes in the laundry basket.

"Your turn," Luck says, climbing into bed. They pull the bun from their hair, long curls exploding into a halo of chestnut brown. My whole apartment fills with the aroma of molasses from their brown sugar conditioner. Luck settles into my side of the bed, not that I'd ever say a word of complaint about it. I'll sleep on the floor if they want.

It takes every effort to pull away from the sight of Luck in my bed and take my own shower. My feet are filthy, the thin suede soles of my dance shoes beyond repair after walking across the roof of the theater in the freezing rain.

But five hundred dollars for the shitty scrap metal, that was barely hanging on by the time I reached it, would mean five hundred less dollars for Twyla and Nisha to keep the theater open. Losing that scrap metal would mean needing more, so the show could go on. And knowing Luck, they'd willingly sacrifice their most treasured connection to their dad for their friends, for the theater where so many of their happy memories were made.

I can't risk losing a single block of wood; I fully intend to return every single nail to Paul the second I can afford the replacement parts after the fundraiser. Working on the roof while nearly naked in the freezing rain and pitch-dark was worth every painful, terrifying second.

Not that the shower is much warmer; Luck left me with lukewarm water and not much of it. I scrub off as quick as I can, the cold egging me on as much as my need to be close to Luck again.

Luck is sitting up against the headboard, waiting for me by the time I finish. I climb into bed next to them, fighting the pride at how long they drink in the sight of my bare chest, how many sidelong glances they steal, thinking I don't notice. We haven't had a proper sleepover since we were in high school. I've crashed at the Alvarez house a few times, less often since I moved out of my parents and into my studio apartment, but Luck and I haven't shared a bed in over a decade.

Strange, how we used to do this every weekend. But after that night senior year...suddenly, our friendship was different. Jorge was always there. Instead of late nights talking in Luck's bed, we camped out in sleeping bags in the basement, with Jorge. I'd assumed Luck wanted a buffer, and that hurt, that they felt we could no longer be friends, just the two of us. I didn't mind his presence, and I've enjoyed becoming Jorge's friend too (he was so much less annoying than Rudy!). But the dynamic we had was forever changed.

Luck nestles into the pillow, rolling on their side to look at me, and my breath catches on my sharp inhale. Their lips, the ones I kissed a mere day ago, are inches from me. The brown eyes I see in my dreams blink slowly. "I'm not mad," they murmur. "About the car."

"You can be, if you are." I roll onto my back, the reminder of why they took so long in the shower making me too ashamed to look at them. "I would be, in your shoes."

"The thing is, if I had been there with you, I probably would have agreed too." They sigh, scooting close enough to rest their cheek on my shoulder. "You said we can return it all?"

"After the fundraiser, if we raise enough to buy new stuff from Melvin," I nod, settling in against them, their skin warm through the borrowed shirt. "Thanks to Rudy's quick thinking, annoyingly."

"Then we do that!" Luck smiles, the cheer in their voice not quite reaching their eyes. "And if not, better the Eldorado than the Firebird. At least Jorge drives his car."

"You won't lose your car," I murmur, finding Luck's hand under the blanket. "I promise."

They lace our fingers together. "I know. I trust you, Felix."

I swallow, my chest bursting as I work up my courage. "About last night..."

"Oh no," Luck groans, and the glow in my chest flickers out. "I don't know if I'm ready to talk about it, but...can I ask you a question?"

"Anything," I say automatically, desperate for any hint of how they might be feeling about that kiss, about me.

"Is my brother," Luck huffs. "Is he straight?"

"What?" I blink, dumbfounded at the unexpected question. What does Jorge have to do with our kiss on Saturday?

"Jorge. Is he straight? Because I thought you two were like..." Luck groans again. "Oh, this is so embarrassing."

This time, that groan makes me laugh. "Are you kidding?"

"I told you you would laugh at me!" Luck buries their face into my shoulder. "Stop it!"

I clap a hand over my mouth, but that just makes me laugh harder. "You thought me and Jorge were...what? Together?"

"Not together! But not *not* together! Not yet, at least!" Luck kicks their feet under the blanket. "I thought you two were, like, pining for each other! For years! But then I realized he might be straight, and my pansexual ass cannot comprehend that at all!"

I turn towards them, still failing to muffle my laughter. "I am pretty sure Jorge's ace. Or at least, somewhere on the ace spectrum. Demi, maybe? You'd really have to ask him. I just mind my own business." A snort escapes me, despite my best efforts. How could Luck possibly think that I was into *Jorge*, instead of them? "Trust me, you would know if he was entertaining anyone. He's got people hitting on him left and right of all genders, and yet, he has never gone on a single date that I'm aware of."

"Really?" Luck asks, brow creasing. "Not anyone?"

"Did you think he was seeing anyone?" I bite my lip, because they seem serious.

They shrug, looking up at me with a bashful smile. "He never brought anyone home, but I thought that's because he wanted *you*. Turns out, I was just being oblivious. I usually am."

"You really are." As if I could be into anyone else, especially Jorge, when I am hopelessly and utterly Luck's. When I have been theirs for years. I press a kiss to their forehead, their cheek, and finally, to their lips.

Our kiss is tender. There's none of the need, the heat, that erupted between us last night. Their lips, and the soft exhale when they part them, are entirely sweet. Entirely perfect.

Tempted as I am to taste their moans again, I fight every instinct to deepen the kiss. Instead, I pull away.

Luck's eyes are closed, lips parted, and it's everything I can do to not dive back in. I might have pushed too far already, when they're still not ready to talk. I stroke their lower lip with my thumb. "Good night, Luck."

Those brown eyes blink open at me. Luck swallows. After a moment, they burrow into my arms, settling in against me with a soft exhale and the sweet scent of molasses that I hope lingers in my sheets forever. "Good night, Felix."

I HAVE NEVER LOVED sleeping more than when I wake up with Luck wrapped around my waist, their long curls in my mouth, legs tangled with mine. The dim morning skies—still gloomy with rain, though gentler now than last night—casts Luck in a muted light, like they're a watercolor painting. But every breath they take, I feel in my own lungs. Every twitch of their hand from their dream leaves me burning through my whole body. The smear of drool on my shoulder is holy water, anointing me with Luck's blessing.

As I lay there, drinking in the bliss of Luck in my arms, I wonder if I should wake them (What time is their first class on Mondays? What time is it anyway?). But I can't bring myself to do it. My alarm hasn't gone off yet; it can't be that late. Maybe I can turn it off telepathically, and we can spend all day in my bed.

Too soon, Luck stirs on their own, and buries their face in my chest with a groan. "You smell *so* fucking good."

"Oh." That was not the grumbled "five more minutes" I expected. Heat flashes through me. Every nerve alights in anticipation as their hand drags up to my waist to pull me closer. Luck's body aligns with mine, their hips rolling as they adjust against me. They let out the quietest whimper when they hitch their leg against me, cunt hot against my hip through the thin fabric of our boxers.

Are they grinding against me on purpose, or is this just sleep-filled affection?

"Good morning," I murmur, stroking their back. The "sit on my face" on the tip of my tongue manages to stay an inside thought. We haven't talked about this yet.

Luck takes a deep breath, then kisses the hollow of my clavicle. "Thank you, for last night. For letting me stay."

So they are awake. My chest tightens with excitement. Luck Alvarez just kissed my neck.

Not because of alcohol, or the heat of the moment, not because I kissed them first.

Because they wanted to.

"Don't go bragging about it," I tease, losing the fight against my grin. It's everything I can do to keep from kicking my feet and squealing, or better idea, kissing Luck senseless all over every inch of their lush body. "Everyone at Sleigh Queen will ask to crash here next time they don't want to drive in the snow."

"I wish you'd let everyone else in town see your sweet side," Luck smiles, the curve of their lips pursing against my bare skin.

"I don't want everyone else in town in my bed, Luck," I murmur, pressing a kiss against their temple. "Just you."

"Felix..." Luck breathes, tilting their head back to look up at me. Their brown eyes are open, lips parted the way they were last night after I kissed them.

This time, I wait for them to close the distance. Every atom in my body hums with anticipation, willing those last few centimeters between us to vanish.

But they don't.

Instead, Luck's lips press together into a smile I've seen thousands of times in our lives, and my heart sinks.

Luck Alvarez has many talents, and none more exemplary than talking themself out of something they want.

Finishing their degree at Julliard? Impossible, according to Luck, accompanied by a sad shrug and a silent warning not to push the subject in front of Jorge, Efrain, and especially not Luis. The younger, more headstrong twin would take matters into his own hands and bully his brothers into moving to Titi Lydia's anyway, because Luck's brothers love their hermane, just as fiercely as Luck loves their brothers.

Reclaiming their dream role as the Sugarplum Fairy in *The Nutcracker*? No, Estelle deserves it more; she's worked so hard to become the prima ballerina she is. Besides, their youngest students love that Luck is Mother Ginger! All said with a wave of their hand, to distract from the longing in their eyes.

Getting upset at me and Jorge for putting their beloved car at risk of being sold for scrap by their piece of shit uncle? No, it's what they would have done, too. Their disappointed sigh hurt worse than any amount of yelling.

Kissing me when they clearly want to?

"I should get to Dancers and Prancers!" Luck chirps, rolling away from me. "Jorge might have lost his key!"

"Luck." I catch their elbow before they can run from this. From me.

"Felix," Luck warns, looking away. Their hand tightens into a fist against the sheet. "I..."

"You need space? Time to think?" I offer, heart clenching at their nod.

But my disappointment doesn't outweigh my hope. While Luck may be good at fooling themself, they're shit at fooling me. Luck will spend however much time they need to convince themself this is a bad idea. For years, I've accepted their word at face value, because they were moving to New York, because they were grieving, because they didn't want me.

But now? Now I know they do.

And I refuse to let Luck talk themself out of our chance to be together again.

"Friday," I murmur. "We're going out."

"Oh? For your birthday?" Luck's voice is too bright, considering they won't look at me.

"Sure," I shrug. I barely remember my own birthday is a mere ten days after theirs, but Luck never forgets. "But no presents."

Luck looks at my hand, still wrapped loosely around their elbow. Not tight enough to keep them from leaving, but they let that hand keep them there, perched on the edge of the bed. "Who all is coming? Do you want me to text out invitations?"

"No. Just you." Sitting up, I let my hand fall from their elbow to their wrist. I pry their fist away from the sheets, and bring it to my lips to kiss the back of their hand. Luck's eyes are wide as they stare at me, each breath a trembling gasp. "Four days, Luck. That's your space, your time. Four days of pretending nothing's changed. Then I'm taking you on a date."

Eleven

Luck

After a long day of classes, I pull up in the garage and start wiping Bertha down. Half paying attention, I keep losing focus as I polish her spokes with a clean rag. Just like I have been all day. Every time I wasn't speaking, I was thinking of Felix. Every time I made a cup of tea reminded me of how he doted on me so carefully last night. Every time I moved, I caught the scent of his soap, of his bed, of him.

I should shower, wash away the sweat of teaching dance all afternoon and my bike ride home. But that would eliminate the musky, fresh smell of something purely Felix embedded into my skin. The intoxicating aroma that had me on the verge of dry humping his leg when I woke up this morning.

Heading up the stairs, I find Jorge and Olive spread out on the couch, watching baseball in the family room. Probably a game he's watched before, analyzing it in some new way I don't understand. Mom used to play when she was young. She signed us all up for T-ball when we were kids. I never quite got the appeal like my brothers did; they all went on to little league, and my parents put me in dance instead.

I was more of my father's kid—gregarious, charming, and always dancing to whatever song he was humming under his breath. He taught us all to dance before we could walk, to live in the moment with endless zeal. Just like how Mom taught us to be intentional, purposeful, driven, to set ourselves up for a bright future. Family meant everything to them.

"Were you ever going to tell me about the deal with Paul about Eldorado?" I ask.

With a muttered curse, Jorge jumps. He pauses the TV, nudging Olive off of his lap. "I should do the dishes."

I open my mouth to tell him I'm not *that* mad, but after a pause, I think better of it. Let him do some chores! Because I am a little mad, not about the deal itself, but that he and Felix never told me. I guess I am also a lot mad at Paul, but I've been a lot mad at Paul for years.

I follow Jorge to the kitchen, and heat up the plate he left me in the microwave. As always, Olive follows the food, while Jorge panic scrubs all of the cups and plates and the scorched pan that's been soaking for two days. I refuse to clean up after a grown man perfectly capable of doing his dishes. Sure, I'll clean up when he cooks for me, which is most evenings because I usually get home late. But that's it. That scorched pan was from some experiment gone awry while I was at the studio, and it's not my job to clean.

Jorge finishes the dishes, while I'm still halfway through the arroz con gandules he made. He dries his hands on a towel, finally admitting, "It's not a good excuse, but I was hoping Felix was gonna tell you."

I freeze mid-bite. "That is literally the worst excuse!" I put my fork down. "You both should have told me. The same day it happened. And yet, neither of you did."

"How did…" Jorge fusses with his curls, leaning against the counter. "How did you find out?"

"Felix let it slip when he was trying to calm me down after—" I wrinkle my nose, not wanting to burden him. But if I want Jorge to keep me in the loop about his mental health, that means being open about mine. "After I had a panic attack at the theater last night."

Jorge's tightening jaw is subtle, but I still catch it. "You okay?"

"Yeah, of course!" I nod. "The power going out during the storm triggered something. That's all." Not to minimize fearing for Felix's life, but I trust him to know his capabilities. I just worry. About him, about everyone dear to me. "And, I'm not mad, about the deal. I mean, I'm pissed at Paul for putting you and Felix in the situation to make the deal in the first place. And I'm mad that neither of you told me about it until just a few days before he might be showing up to take the Eldorado from me—"

"He won't!" Jorge sits down at the table across from me. "We have until after the show. Felix will figure it out."

"I know." I believe it, wholeheartedly. Felix wouldn't let Paul get away with it. None of us would, except Titi Lydia, who loves peace and stability more than she loves us. "I just would appreciate some time to make a backup plan, or mentally prepare myself for a huge emotional blow."

"You don't need a backup plan!" Jorge shakes his head. "You have Felix. He'll figure it out," he repeats, as if reassuring himself more than me.

"He always does," I chuckle, because I know he will. Still, I don't want to rely on Felix to solve all of my problems. Anytime I need him, he is there. No matter what I need, or what burden I put on him, he is ready and willing to bend over backwards for me. I shake my head. How had I been so blind to his feelings for me? I put my chin in my hand and frown at my brother. "So what's up with your sexual orientation these days?"

Jorge's jaw hangs open as he processes my question. "What?"

"Are you straight? Bi? Ace? Some other label?"

With a groan, Jorge pulls his hoodie up over his curls. "Why are you asking me this?"

"Don't laugh," I wave my fork in warning. "But until Saturday, I thought you were in love with Felix."

Despite my warning not to, Jorge smothers a quiet laugh with his hand.

"I said don't laugh!" I scoff, which only makes his giggles worse. "I only realized I might be wrong when I saw how awkward you were around Estelle and Junie." To my delight, my brother stops laughing, and pulls the strings of his hoodie tight with another groan. "But then, Felix said you don't really date anyone, and he's just been assuming you're ace until you tell him otherwise. So now I don't know what to think. So, are you straight? Or ace? Or what?"

"Question." Jorge raises his hand. "What's ace?"

"Asexual?" I reply, confused. "Or perhaps aromantic, if that's a more accurate label for you. Or both?"

"Can you use it in a sentence?" Jorge teases. "Wait no, can I have the definition?"

"Do you really not know this?" I ask. Maybe I'm more hip to queer lingo than I thought, if this isn't common knowledge for Jorge. I've always assumed he was some flavor of bisexual too, even if he never came out officially (teenage Jorge made Frank Ocean his whole personality after he came out). "Ace means you don't experience much, if any, attraction to other people. Sexual for ace, or romantic for aro, or both? You may even be repulsed by the idea of sex and-slash-or relationships?"

"I don't think that sounds quite right, but I guess it doesn't sound wrong?" Jorge shrugs. "Like, I'm not straight, but do I have to call myself something?"

"No, of course not!" I shovel some arroz in my mouth. "I was just curious."

"Just curious, or you just want to make the conversation about me, so you can avoid the inevitable question of how the fuck you thought I was in love with Felix this whole time?" Jorge snorts.

I scoff. Read for filth by my own brother. "You said you had a crush on him!"

"Yeah, in ninth grade!" Jorge's shoulders shake as he buries his face in his hands. "Mom kept trying to get me to bring a date to the homecoming dance. Felix was safe to pick because he was already going with you!"

"As friends!"

"Sure, yeah, as friends." Jorge snorts. "Besides, Felix was the only person I knew well enough to not be completely disgusted with dancing and kissing if my plan backfired—" He pauses. "Hey, maybe I am ace, or whatever."

"So you just...haven't dated anyone?" I ask around a big bite of rice. Olive is creeping closer, her tail thumping against the table leg. I have about three minutes before she starts begging aggressively, and this has onions and chilis and stuff she should not be eating.

"I've dated!" Jorge crosses his arms, leaning back in his chair. "I took Estelle to homecoming senior year, and we were talking for a few weeks, but then the accident..." He trails off with a wave of his hand. "She ended up going to prom with fucking *Rudy* instead. She downgraded."

"You were dating *my* Estelle?" A surge of protectiveness for my prima ballerina races through me. "And Rudy? Is he queer too? I thought she transitioned after high school?"

"I don't know shit about *that* jackass," Jorge sneers. "But no, Estelle was out in high school. At least in school, she was. Maybe not to everyone in town, though."

"What about since after the accident? You dated anyone lately?" I prompt, lifting my foot just as Olive tries to jump into the chair next to me. "Off! This is my food!"

Jorge smirks, hiding his eyes. "I made out with Junie at Sleigh Queen last weekend. She was just trying to make Rudy jealous, though."

"What?" I cry. Rice flies out from my mouth, and Olive is licking my lap before I can stop her. "How do you know that?"

"Because she asked if she could make out with me to make Rudy jealous." Jorge snickers. "Is that still ace? Because I kind of enjoyed that. Making out with his situationship to piss him off. Besides, it seemed to do the job. They disappeared upstairs in the lounge, and I went home."

"I think I want to know less about all of this, actually." I shove the empty plate to the middle of the table. Olive yips at me and stomps her feet. "Why are you and Rudy getting involved with my students? Leave them alone!"

"I have been the perfect gentleman!" Jorge presses a hand to his chest. "And Junie initiated all of that. I just agreed to it! Enthusiastically!"

"You made out with her purely to piss off your best friend's little brother." I raise an eyebrow at him. "Nothing about this sounds straight, or ace."

Jorge laughs. "You see why Felix hasn't asked about my sexuality now? I'm an unlabeled man of mystery!"

"Do you want me to set you up with someone who isn't a student of mine?" I rub my temples. "I've heard Ara rejected Rudy, if that's what does it for you."

"No!" Jorge frowns, all traces of amusement leaving his face. "You're not my parent, Luck. My love life, of lack thereof, is not your responsibility."

My eyebrows shoot up as I scoff. "It might be nice for you to date more—"

"If you even think about setting me up on a single date, I will train Olive to steal your shoes," Jorge warns. Olive tippy-taps around the table at the sound of her name. "You know I'll do it. No baseball mitt in this house has been safe since Luis tried to prank me that one time. Poor Efrain caught a stray with that trick."

I raise my hands in surrender. "She's still throwing her food bowl at my head every morning."

"That was Luis who taught her that, not me!" Jorge rubs Olive's ears. "She did it to me this morning, since you weren't here." He smirks knowingly, then softens. "It wasn't just my fake teenage crush on Felix that got in your way, was it?"

"I thought it was real," I murmur, burning with embarrassment. "Not just a crush."

"Why?" he asks. "He and I are friends, always have been. He's been in love with you since high school!"

With a sigh, I stand, putting my plate in the sink as I dig out everything I'll need for Mom's hot chocolate recipe. The second the cheese is in my hand, Olive is on my heels. "Bed, Olive." I nod to the dog bed in the corner of the kitchen. The stove ignites blue under the pan, and I break off the chocolate in chunks. "You only collect the tax if you're good."

Ears perked up, Olive flies to her bed, flopping down hard enough to knock the wind out of her. Her tail never slows.

"I think it was an excuse at first." I whisk the cinnamon and cloves in with the melting chocolate. "Because I was going to New York, and I was afraid that if Felix and I started something, we would break up, and I would lose my best friend for good."

Pulling out the cutting board, Jorge silently dices the cheese next to the stove.

"But then you two got so close while I was there," I shake my head, pouring the milk slowly into the pan as I whisk it together. Titi Lydia says we should use water, but Mom always made it with milk. "After I moved back, everything he used to be with me, he was for you." I fight the surge of bitter jealousy I'd smothered years and years ago, when I came downstairs to find a recovering Jorge cradled in Felix's arms as they slept in my brother's bed. The easy kisses they'd exchange to each other's cheeks and foreheads. The way Jorge seemed to turn to Felix for emotional support, instead of me. How Felix put Jorge's well-being above everything. "It felt like I'd lost him, too. But you needed him more than I did after the accident, with the panic attacks and everything, so I just walled everything up."

Jorge puts an arm around me.

I smile, leaning into him. "I managed, because I had to. Because you, Efrain, and Luis needed me to. Felix and I eventually became close again, but you two were still so..." I sigh. "I just assumed that you two felt for each other the way I felt about Felix, and did my best to accept that. I didn't want to get in the way."

"It was never like that with us." Jorge keeps his arm around my shoulders, dropping the cheese into mugs for us with his other hand. "The panic attacks, they started before the accident. I didn't have anyone who understood what I was dealing with after you moved to New York. Mom and Dad didn't get it, because they didn't want to accept that they put so much on your shoulders, more than any kid should have to deal with. I don't know how you handled *everything* when you were so young. They relied on you so much, and then when you moved to New York, they needed to rely on me. I couldn't do a fraction of what you did."

I rest my head on his shoulder. It's easy to have rose-colored glasses for our parents, because I only want to remember the good about them. But Jorge's right; they could be a little toxic too, only ever acknowledging the good, not the bad. Never thanking me for what they saw as my responsibility. I hadn't realized they parentified Jorge so much in my absence.

"Felix still came over for dinner sometimes after you went to college, and he saw how everything started falling apart. How *I* started falling apart." Jorge takes the pan, pouring the steaming chocolate into our mugs. "And he helped. Both around the house, and with the twins, and keeping me grounded when I thought I would lose it. Yeah, we grew close, but as friends, brothers—never anything romantic." He sets the pan down. "You just saw us after the accident, when he helped with my nightmares and physical therapy and anything he could to make your life easier. He was basically my Olive, I guess? Before we got Olive, and then I didn't need him as much. Yeah, he was helping me, and our family, because he loves us too. But it's always been for *you*, Luck."

Leaning against the kitchen counter, I sip my hot cocoa, letting the rich, creamy flavor calm me, the way it always did as a kid. It should be harder to wrap my head around what Jorge is saying. But I simply nod and murmur, "I know."

Because I do know that. I've always known that. I just didn't want to risk losing the person who understands, supports, *loves* me more than anyone. After so much grief and sacrifice, Felix is someone I can no longer afford to lose. He is all I have left of the future I once dreamed of, where we could both be free to chase the lives we wanted. Where our families would be thriving without relying on us, and we could be ourselves, together, wherever we ended up.

But then Felix told me he wouldn't be applying to college at all; the Kellys couldn't afford it. And then every time I came home for Christmas or summer, he changed more and more, until he was someone I didn't know anymore. Not in terms of gender, because I loved seeing him so happy; we just...grew apart. We went from being glued at the hip and doing everything together, to having completely separate lives. He had my brother to replace me. At least, that's how it felt. Like my parents, I can be too focused on what I want to be true, what I *need* to be true, that I don't let myself accept what is right in front of me.

The truth of the matter is, Felix didn't go anywhere. I did. I left, and I changed too. I lived the life I wanted, always hoping Felix would follow me. Follow the dreams we both shared, when he could. Then I moved back here, and I had to figure out how to reconcile the Luck I'd become with the life Lucia left behind, all while grieving my parents and being the support my brothers needed. Felix was there for me through it all, even though he didn't know me as well anymore.

I take another sip, chuckling half-heartedly into my mug as Jorge makes Olive earn her cheese tax, rolling over, sitting pretty, and putting the trash in the bin, before he finally sets it on her nose. The second the cheese cube hits her mouth, she zoomies around like a mad dog, knocking over a dining chair as she whirls in tornados around the kitchen.

This is my year of processing everything, isn't it? Of moving on from grief, of accepting the loss of the life I'd dreamed of, of leaning into the joy I have. All these years of keeping Felix at arm's length, but unwilling to let him go, and Felix is still here for me, still waiting for me to pull him close. Maybe there's still hope for one of my lost dreams.

Twelve

Felix

"What happened to the rest?" I ask Dad, staring at the crates of empty beer bottles that he's accumulated this week. "Normally there's a couple dozen more."

Is Dad actually cutting back on his drinking, like he always says he will? I was counting on this bottle deposit to help scrape together enough for their water bill that's past due, but if we can save money by buying one less case this week, that would do it too.

"Oh, Rudy already brought them out to the garage!" Dad waves the spatula at me, dancing along to the radio as he browns some ground beef for the spaghetti he's making. "We had too many, and they were cluttering up the kitchen. Your mom started drinking some fancy kombucha stuff. Smells awful!" He says the last bit extra loud, grinning at me when my mom scoffs from the living room.

"You smell awful!" Mom teases back from her recliner. "The Thriving with Chronic Fatigue Facebook group says it's supposed to be good for my digestion with this new medication the doctor has me on!"

Another thing they can't afford. Great. I heft the crates up off the floor to bring them to my truck. If kombucha and this new trial drug helps her feel better, then it's worth it. And we will manage, like we always do. "Rude!" I call up the stairs. "Come help me with these bottles!"

"Eat shit!" my brother calls back.

"Need a hand, bud?" Dad offers from the fridge as he pulls out a beer.

"No, just want someone to help me return these." I lift the crates, bottles rattling inside. "Dinner's burning."

"Oh, right!" Dad laughs, "I'm cooking!"

Rudy comes downstairs with some folded kitchen towels, tucking them away in the drawer, before he opens the door to the garage for me. "Dad, what are you forgetting?"

Dad waves him off, grabbing a lid for the sauce simmering on the stove. "I know! I know! Keep it covered, keep it clean!"

"I don't want to clean marinara off the ceiling again!" Rudy teases.

I exhale slowly as I escape into the garage. I love our parents, but I could not live with them. I don't know how Rudy does it. Before I moved out, Dad and I argued at least once a week, big shouting matches about money or his drinking or how irresponsible he can be. I made Mom cry several times, and Rudy and I bickered constantly. My little brother might be an annoying little shit, but he handles them better than I can. He has a way of getting them to do what they need to do, without hurting their feelings the way I unintentionally do.

He shouldn't have to, though. Rudy should be able to move out and grow up. To figure out his own life, without worrying that he's abandoning them.

We load the crates and boxes into the truck in silence, climb in, and head into town. The way we have dozens of times, and at least once a month since I moved into my apartment eight years ago.

Our regular trip to the grocery store to get the deposits back on the beer bottles, to the next town to sell scrap metal, is my way of giving Rudy a break. He's the only thing standing between my parents' lives falling apart. They're so happy, so in love, that they're always content with accepting less than they deserve. Rudy's the same way; content with the cards he's been dealt, never dreaming bigger. At least, not that he's shared with me.

Not that I'm one to talk. I still work for Dad, still have never left this weirdly cheerful small town, still have nothing to show for myself except a messy apartment. That's enough for me. I have a community at Sleigh Queen, friends like the Alvarezes, Twyla, and Nisha. I have Luck, who slept in my bed last night and kissed my neck this morning.

"So how's the stripping?" Rudy asks, out of the blue.

I shoot him a look. We normally don't talk during our outings. "Fine."

"You have fun? Learning a lot?" Rudy smiles innocently.

"What the fuck are you talking about?" I frown, turning back to the road as we turn down Figgy Pudding Avenue to the grocery store.

"Just wondering!" Rudy shrugs, still with that weird smirk on his face. "Making conversation with my brother, you know. Chatting about your life."

"Well, if you want to know..." I give him one more suspicious look, not believing him for a second. "I'm enjoying it a lot. It's nice, to dance with Luck again."

"I bet it is!" Rudy teases suggestively.

"Shut the fuck up, dipwad," I frown. "I didn't mean like that. It's just...like how we used to dance together, when we were young. Only better than it was back then. And I get why Luck likes teaching, now that I'm basically part of their class. Like you remember that Evans kid I used to babysit?"

"Uh..." Rudy thinks. "Oh, Avery? Yeah."

"Yeah, remember how they didn't talk, like at all, until they were in middle school?"

"Uh huh. They still barely talk. They just stare at me until I get creeped out and leave."

"Well, they're in the class, and they are just...flourishing?" I grimace. "That sounds cheesy. But they are! They're outgoing and chatty and enthusiastic. And yeah, it's a little weird that it took a burlesque class to pull them out of their shell, especially since I used to babysit them—and Nome for that matter—but it's cool, seeing the impact Luck has on everyone. Like, Junie and Estelle are complete opposites in personality, but they're super tight now."

"What do they say about me?" Rudy blurts out.

Sucking my teeth, I pull into the parking lot of Wynter's Wonderland Market. "Did you ask me how class was going so I would tell you what Junie and Estelle think about you?"

"No!" Rudy scoffs. "Maybe."

"Which one?" I ask, putting the truck in park. Neither of us makes a move to get out, and I'm so glad we got here just in time for me to watch him squirm. Rudy stares at the dashboard, cheeks reddening. "Estelle, or Junie?"

"Both! Either!" Rudy shrugs, too casually.

I cross my arms. "I'll tell you what *one* of them said about you, but you have to pick."

Rudy considers it. "Well, I already know what Junie thinks of me, so Estelle?" He pauses. "Wait, no, Junie. Dammit. Yeah, Junie."

"Final answer?" I am loving this. Who knew this class would give me a new way to torture my brother?

Rudy nods.

I smirk. "Nothing."

"What?" Rudy blanches.

"Junie has not said one single word about you." I turn off the engine and unbuckle. "How's that feel? Hurts, I bet, doesn't it?"

"What about Estelle, then?" Rudy grabs my arm. "What'd she say about me?"

"You really want to know?" I wince.

"Yes!" Rudy's face is bright red now.

"Come here," I lean in, gesturing for him to come closer. When my brother does, I swat the back of his head, "Also nothing!"

"God damn, you are such an ass!" Rudy groans, punching my shoulder.

I punch his right back. "Yeah, well, you need to get your shit together more before you start chasing anyone, let alone grown women with standards like Junie and Estelle. You're twenty-five, dude. They deserve better than some fuckboy handyman."

"Is that why you still haven't made a move on Luck?" Rudy snarks.

My blood runs hot, and I jump out of the cab. The cold spring breeze is a balm against the irritation buzzing under my skin. "Shut the fuck up. You don't know what the fuck you're talking about."

"And neither do you!" Rudy hops out too, slamming the passenger door behind him. "At least tell Luck that you have feelings for them. Please! Put us all out of your misery!"

I frown. This isn't the shit-talking I was expecting from him. "That almost sounded like genuine advice."

Rudy snorts, opening the bed of the pickup. "Look, even though it's really fucking obvious to everyone else, Luck can be really oblivious."

"Understatement," I snort. I hope I've made myself pretty clear the past couple days, but knowing Luck and how their brain will jump through hoops to keep their heart safe, I'll need to keep making myself clear. "Don't worry about me, Rude, but thanks for the attempt at telling me what to do."

"Yeah, well, you've been a sad, pining simp forever. It's getting a little pathetic."

"Jackass," I mutter, hauling the crates into a nearby cart.

"Assface," Rudy returns, filling his own cart.

I'm strangely tempted to tell Rudy about this weekend, that things between Luck and I have shifted, gaining momentum more quickly than I ever expected. But if I tell my brother, he'll tell our parents, and Dad will tell god-knows-who, and everyone in this town is nosy enough as it is. I need to make sure Luck and I are on the same page, because if we're about to blow up our friendship, it won't be to scratch an itch. My heart couldn't handle that.

However, after last night, for the first time, I truly believe Luck might feel the same. For years, I've put everyone ahead of myself, no one more than Luck. My whole life, I've been what everyone has needed from me, in all the ways I can give without losing myself. Now I have an opportunity to be what *I* need, to go after what *I* want.

If Luck is having their year of growth and healing and all that, why can't I?

Fourteen

Luck

True to his word, for the next four days, Felix acts like nothing has changed. He texts me like normal, mostly memes and the occasional update about Sleighbell Stage, including the good news that the insurance company approved the theater to reopen for our performance tomorrow. I'm annoyed that he manages to turn off his intensity and charm like they never existed, as much as I'm relieved for the space. How can he simply pretend he didn't turn my world upside down last weekend? Why am I so nervous for tonight?

Catching my curls in the diffuser, I stare into the overflowing mess of my closet. I have no idea what to expect. Felix said to wear whatever I wanted, but...this is a date. Right? My usual joggers and messy bun won't cut it.

However, it's also Sleighbell Springs. We're a Christmas town, not some high-end glam tourist destination. There are no bougie restaurants or cocktail bars. It's a town of cute date spots, not sweeping romantic gestures and private candlelit dinners.

Then again, if we were just hanging out like normal, he wouldn't have sent me home to get ready after the dress rehearsal. He wouldn't have murmured that he'll pick me up at eight when he hugged me goodbye, quiet enough that everyone else couldn't hear. He wouldn't have given me that lingering look that promised so much more than dinner before we left the theater. Until a week ago, I never pegged Felix as a sweeping romantic gesture kind of guy. He's always been a rough-around-the-edges grump. Flannel and determination and a quiet, proud aura.

But then he kissed my hand like Mr. Fucking Darcy last weekend, and my head hasn't stopped spinning since. My heart has been fluttering like I'm sixteen again, and Felix is triggering my queer awakening while we try our one and only cigarette in the gym locker room. The exhilaration of hiding in a shower stall together, muffling each other's laughter when we almost got caught. The way Felix's lips pursed around the filter sparked such an overpowering need in me that I resolved to never smoke again, because that feeling was uncontrollable and terrifying.

Today when we danced together...it was like we were young again. Completely in sync, like we could read each other's mind. With every microexpression, I knew exactly what he wanted. Felix picked up on my ideas before I could say them aloud, already moving into place to catch me from my spin, or change that simple step to a foxtrot.

All of that tension, the distance, the fumbling, faltering starts and stops that have plagued us the past few weeks, are gone. Even with our mistakes, we recover together, as if whoever messed up intended to do so from the start. Our final dress rehearsal earlier this afternoon flowed so beautifully, and I can't help but wish it's because we've finally stopped holding back.

For our date, I settle on a wool pantsuit I bought in a thrift store back when I lived in New York. It's a boring navy, but the high waistline and the double breasted brass buttons means I don't need to wear anything other than a bra under it. I choose a bright red lace bustier, barely visible under the collar of the jacket. The shoulder pads are probably unflattering by conventional standards, considering I'm short and curvy, but they make me feel powerful.

Knowing Felix, he'll probably just wear a nicer flannel. Already, this is better dressed than anything I ever need to wear in Sleighbell Springs, but I feel good in it. The lining is silky against my skin.

After touching up my lip gloss and mascara, I slip my duck boots on. They feel clunky and heavy on my feet, given how nice my outfit is. However, it's March in Vermont; the slush is ankle-deep in some spots. Felix won't judge me for being practical, and he said we could walk to town together, so I don't need to psyche myself up for a car ride.

A Ho Ho Handyman truck pulls in the driveway, right on time, just as I'm buttoning up my jacket. I open the door, blinking in surprise. Out the corner of my eye, Rudy waves as he backs out of the driveway, honking obnoxiously.

But I can't drag my eyes away from Felix. He wears a peacoat and a scarf that I knitted him years ago, when I thought a new hobby would help the seasonal depression. His red curls are styled as classily as a mullet can be, his mustache and beard neatly trimmed.

Felix stuffs his hands in his pockets, blue eyes lingering on my exposed chest, before snapping back up to my face. "Ready?"

I nod, falling into step beside him.

He takes my hand and stuffs it into his pocket with his.

Heat rushes to my cheeks as our fingers lace together in the deep warmth of his coat pocket. "Is holding hands part of the date?"

"Yup," is his only reply.

"Okay." I bite back my smile as we head toward downtown. It's sweet, that he insisted on picking me up without driving. I offered to meet him somewhere, but Felix wouldn't hear of it. He comes across as such a jerk sometimes, but he's the kindest person I know.

"Happy birthday, Felix," I murmur, squeezing his hand.

"One of these years, I'll catch up to you." He shoots me a teasing smirk.

I laugh; that was our first real argument. When I gloated about turning six a whole ten days before him, Felix took that as a personal challenge. "That's not how birthdays work."

"Yeah-huh."

"Nah-uh."

"Wanna bet?"

"You're such an Aries, Felix."

"Gonna cry about it, water sign?"

Our familiar banter carries us all the way down past Mistletoe Street as Felix leads us to the Reindeer Roadhouse. It's a charming, quaint restaurant, and the food is always amazing, but not the private birthday date spot I was envisioning. The hubbub of the dining room is a constant murmur, even late on a Friday evening.

Felix nods at the hostess before leading me to the upper level, usually reserved for private events. It's quiet, with only the crackle of the fireplace to set the ambiance.

"What are we doing up here?" I ask, stunned to see a single table set in front of the fireplace, candles already lit, a bottle of champagne on ice. My heart flutters. I never expected any spot in Sleighbell Springs to be this romantic. "Felix, you rented out the whole event space? You didn't spend a lot of money on this, did you? You didn't need to—"

"Luck," Felix silences me with one quiet murmur of my name and a gentle hand on my arm. "I am a pushover handyman, and this family-owned restaurant is a hundred years old. Let's just say the Reindeer Roadhouse owed me a few favors." He pulls out the chair for me, motioning me to sit. "But even if they didn't, I invited you on this date, and you don't need to worry about how I'm paying for it. Just enjoy, and let me spoil you how you deserve."

I pull my coat off, and sit. "Fine. Sorry for caring about your budget."

Felix snorts, pulling off his own coat. "You're not sorry at all."

"I'm not. In fact I'll probably—" I freeze when Felix turns around. His crisp, sky blue button down matches his eyes. The buttons are undone enough to show off the musculature of his chest. "...do it again," I finish in a whisper, dragging my gaze up his veiny neck that took every ounce of willpower not to bite on Monday morning when I woke up in his bed, wrapped around him from head to toe, and yet still wishing I could be closer.

Fuck, I am so gone for this man.

The server, Cindy Cane (Aiden's older sister, and a classmate of ours from high school, because everyone knows everyone in this town) walks in with a tray of food. "Not to be weird about this," Cindy waves her hand between us once she sets down the platter on the tray stand. "But I am so excited for you two. May asked me to get a statement for her gossip column, if you have anything you'd like to share, on the record."

"What?" Felix deadpans. I merely blink, wholly unsurprised that somehow our date is common knowledge already.

"You know, the whole town has been waiting for this to happen for years! I personally thought it would happen prom night senior year, but we can't win 'em all!" Cindy winks, setting down the soup course in front of us. "So, anything to say, for the Gazette? Or if you prefer to stay off the record, I can say it comes from a close source."

"Absolutely not," Felix shakes his head.

"So no photo?" Cindy pulls her phone out of her apron.

"No!" Felix grumbles. "Can we get a new server? I asked for a table up here so we could have privacy."

"Hun, you're not paying for this," Cindy retorts, unwrapping the champagne foil with a raised eyebrow.

"Guess I'll just take back the window I replaced last month," Felix mutters. "For free!"

"I have something for May," I smile. "On the record."

Felix groans.

"Ooh, I knew I could count on you, Luck!" Cindy beams, popping the cork.

"You can tell May North to mind her own business." I grin at Felix's laugh.

Cindy simply beams harder as she fills our flutes. "You two are so perfect for each other! Just remember the sign, my little lovebirds!" She points at the placard above the fireplace that reads, *Please no sex in front of the fireplace for sanitary and legal purposes.* "I'll be back with your mains soon!"

My cheeks are hot, because while I hadn't considered the option of sex in front of the fireplace before, now I want to. "You ordered champagne?" I ask instead, as soon as she's out of earshot. Safer topic to discuss than imagining my bare ass on the table, while Felix feasts on me instead of dinner.

"It's a special occasion." Felix gives me a soft smile, a twinkle in his blue eyes that hints he's reading my mind again.

Or perhaps my fantasy is as plain as day on my face. A more likely option, considering how tempted I am to dunk my whole head in the ice bucket. "But you don't drink."

Felix sits back in his chair, eyebrow raised. "I don't drink when I'm driving. I don't drink to excess. I don't drink when I'm alone. I don't drink to make social situations easier," Felix lists off his many reasons for not drinking. "But here, with you, on my birthday, when I fully plan on taking you back to my place after this—" His blue eyes go wide as he gapes, rushing to add, "If you're up for that, of course, I'm happy to walk you home if you prefer!" He rubs his forehead with a sigh. "I don't see the risk in a glass or two."

Heat rushes through me at the idea of spending another night with Felix—perhaps one where he kisses me properly this time. Perhaps one where we don't stop at kissing. I raise my glass. "Happy birthday, Felix Kelly."

He clinks his glass with mine. Our eyes stay locked over our sip of the sweet bubbles.

Felix wrinkles his nose. "*That's* champagne? That's...not what I expected. That's apple juice. Fizzy, gross apple juice."

"It's not for everyone, but it's nice on special occasions." I laugh, taking my first taste of the creamy potato and leek soup in front of us. The flavor is bright and hearty, a perfect blend of winter and spring. "So, any birthday wishes?"

Felix dips a crust of bread into the soup. "A few."

"Care to elaborate?" I tease. "Knowing you, you're already making them happen."

"Well, yeah!" Felix gestures with his bread, like it should be obvious. "Wishes are one thing, but plans are another."

"Spoken like a true Aries," I snort. "Let me hear these plans."

His gaze drops to his food as he hesitates. "I want to start my own contracting company. Not to compete with my dad's business, but to do shit like repair the community theater, the kind of stuff that takes a little more forethought and certifications than my dad can manage. Not that he's bad at his work, but..."

"He's not you," I murmur, dragging a slice of bread through the soup. "He's content getting by. And you're not."

"Exactly," Felix nods. "I don't want to scramble for rent every month. I don't want to have to make shady deals with your uncle to get the parts I need. I want to have some credibility with everyone else in town, not pity or sympathy." The corner of his lips tug into a crooked smile. "I want to be able to spoil you rotten, without having to call in favors."

My cheeks burn as I swallow the bite of bread. "You don't have to spoil me—"

"But I *want* to. Because your martyr ass puts everyone else before you." Felix's voice is firm. "If you thought I was into *Jorge* all these years—"

"Jorge is a catch!" I insist, burning with embarrassment all over again.

"I'm sure he'll make someone very happy, if he wants that," Felix concedes, his blue eyes flicking up to mine. "But he's not you, Luck."

I swallow, my mouth going dry as my heart flutters in my chest.

"I won't pressure you, because I know you wouldn't put up with any of my bossy ass bullshit, anyway," Felix smirks, and I can't help but smile with him. "And you probably want more space to think things through. I'm happy to give you as much as you need, take everything as slow as you want." He pauses, resting his hand on the table, palm up. An invitation to take it. "But I want to show you what you deserve, if you let me. Let me give you what we both want, even if it means letting someone put you first, for once. That's my real birthday wish."

"You're not supposed to say what you wish for out loud. It's bad luck." Heart in my throat, I fight against the instinct to downplay my feelings, to deny the surge of desire that burns through me. I've spent so long pretending everything is fine, that I'm happy and content. But Felix has seen through it. He's waited years for me to be ready for him, for us. "But since that's what you want for your birthday, and you wouldn't let me buy you a present..." I slide my hand across the table to rest it in his.

Felix's quiet laugh is the most beautiful sound I've ever heard.

Fifteen

Felix

In every scenario that's played through my head the past few days, I expected to have to coax Luck more. But no, once they got over their wide-eyed trepidation during the first course, Luck has been unexpectedly...chill, for lack of a better word.

Even now, as we walk down Mistletoe Street, their hand is laced with mine, in my pocket again like this is completely normal for us. Like we've been together for years, instead of this being our first date. No hesitant movements or awkward lulls in our conversation. Just us, together, the way I've always hoped for. As we walk, Luck leans against me, the lights strung along the evergreen-lined Mistletoe Street reflecting in their dark eyes like stars.

"Too bad it's not Christmas." Luck smiles when they catch me staring at them, instead of the festive sights in our picturesque town. "It'd be fun to go ice skating."

"If it were Christmas, we'd be working," I remind them. "I'd be trying to keep kids from crying on Santa's lap all day, and then trying to pry thirsty gays *out* of Santa's lap at Sleigh Queen all night."

Luck laughs. "And you'd love every minute."

I grumble, but I do enjoy it. A little.

"Stop pretending to be a Scrooge, you big softy!" Luck elbows me. "You wouldn't be head elf every year if you weren't great with kids. Or thirsty gays."

"They just hire me 'cause I'm short."

"You can't be short because we're the same height!" Luck smiles. "They hire you because your legs look fantastic in tights."

I can't help but snort. Luck always hypes up how attractive their friends are. But still, my face warms, because they noticed my legs.

Luck stops me as we approach the Sleighbell Stage, where Twyla is updating the marquee to add a "SOLD OUT!" under our show name.

"Sold out?" Luck squeals. Twyla jumps at the sound, but the ladder is steady underneath her. "That's amazing!"

"As of a few hours ago, yup! And we got all the inventory for the silent auction and raffle set up for tomorrow!" Twyla calls from the top of the ladder. "Thanks to you, Luck, we might just make it to next Christmas."

The knot of anxiety in my chest that's been sitting like a lump since Luck first asked me to help, almost three weeks ago, loosens ever so slightly. But there's still so much to figure out between the insurance payments, and getting Paul's shitty scrap metal back to him by Sunday morning, without risking the Eldorado.

And somehow starting my own business so the insurance company can pay me, not my dad. Because I said it out loud to Luck, and they're going to make me follow through. Good thing I already filed the request to open a new business with the Chamber of Holiday Cheer. I don't need their approval to register with the state, but if I want to do business with anyone in Sleighbell Springs, I need the Chamber's approval. Unfortunately, with Luck's uncle Paul on the council, I'm facing an uphill battle. Hopefully I can convince someone to bring it up for a vote without his gatekeeping. And cross my fingers they'll approve it, despite the blatantly uncheerful business name.

At least I'm not worried about our performance. Our rehearsals this week have been like a dream, like we haven't gone over a decade without dancing together. Even our dress rehearsal today—our first and only run through with May and the other queens from Sleigh Queen (Dee Pression and Dixie Normous have joined the lineup, and Tucker Envy and Carlyle volunteered to bartend), the pole dancers, and the aerialists who are performing with us—was easier than I expected. Everyone did what they needed to do, and other than a few minor mishaps, everything went fine.

Hand still in mine, Luck drags me across the street—claiming it'd be bad luck to walk under the marquee when the sign is being changed, because it's basically walking under a ladder—as we head toward my apartment.

"Was there something else you wanted to do?" I ask, once we're out of earshot from Twyla. I had assumed, had *hoped*, we would head back to my place. To talk, to hang out, perhaps to make out a bit, if they want. Or more than a bit. But then they suggested ice skating, and now I'm doubting that plan. "Wrong time of year to take you ice skating, but we can go see a movie, or get hot cocoa, or something. Bookstore?"

Luck stops in their tracks. "Felix!"

Concerned at how serious their tone is, I turn toward them, humming in surprise when they grab my scarf to pull me into a kiss. As shock sinks into blissful disbelief, I melt into them. Luck Alvarez is kissing me, out in the open, in the middle of Mistletoe Street, where anyone walking by might see us.

"Twelve years, Felix," they murmur against my lips. "Twelve fucking years, I wanted to do this again." My heart surges as they slowly back me against the wall of the Candy Cane Cafe, one hand cradling the crown of my head, before their tongue teases the seam of my mouth. I part my lips, drawing in a shuddering breath. But

Luck pauses, their dark eyes teasing as they flick down to where I'm gasping for them, desperate for more. "I don't want to go to a movie, or a bookstore, or even ice skating, Felix. I want you to give me what we both want."

"What?" I pant, my mind spinning. A kiss from Luck is far more intoxicating than the glass of sickly sweet champagne I had with dinner. "This whole time? You said you didn't like me."

Twelve years ago, we were eighteen. Seniors in high school, celebrating our dance team's championship win at state. The Alvarezes hosted the party where Luck and I found ourselves alone in the backyard, watching the fire together, when everyone else went inside.

When Luck leaned their head on my shoulder that night, I took my chance.

Luck would later chalk that kiss up to the excitement of the moment, that it hadn't meant anything when they kissed me back. For me, that kiss was an act of courage. Years of secretly pining for my best friend, never knowing if they felt the same way. It crushed me when Luck told me they didn't like me back, that the kiss was a mistake. The distance Luck put between us after that hurt more than words could say. But after being rejected so soundly, Jorge's constant presence was a welcome buffer.

"I *couldn't* like you, Felix," Luck murmurs, stepping away, leaving me panting against the wall. "I was about to move to New York, and what if changing everything between us meant I lost you? Lost my best friend?" They huff. "And Jorge's crush on you wasn't exactly subtle."

"It was incredibly subtle!" I retort, still in disbelief that Luck has kept me at arm's length for so long for the sake of their *brother*. A grown adult, who has been in enough therapy to handle his own feelings, if he did, in fact, have a crush on me. Which he did not. "Because it didn't exist!"

Luck raises an eyebrow. "Agree to disagree?"

"No, but fine." It takes everything in me not to argue back, because in the end, it doesn't matter if Jorge did or did not have a crush on me; Luck believed he did. "But for the record, that kiss, the one twelve years ago, I meant it. It wasn't us getting caught up in the moment. I liked you, Luck. And I still do."

"I know," they murmur. "I'm sorry for minimizing it. I didn't mean to hurt you, I was just...protecting myself. Because I did like you, I just couldn't afford to. I talked myself out of it so hard, I convinced myself that my feelings weren't real." Luck holds out their hand, nodding toward my apartment. I take it, shoving our hands back in my pocket, so their fingers don't get cold in the half a block left of our walk. "I tried so hard to get over you, Felix. I dated around a bit in New York, but no one ever compared to how I felt about you." Their voice cracks as their breath hitches. "And after my parents passed..."

"I know," I murmur as I pull them into a hug, squeezing until their breathing deepens. After a quick kiss pressed to their cheek, I fish my key out of my pocket to let us into the door tucked next to the Tatted Nutcracker that leads to my studio apartment upstairs. I hold the door open to let Luck pass. "And now?"

"Now, I'm tired of pretending I don't want you." Luck shrugs their coat off as they race up the stairs, flashing a smirk over their shoulder. "And I want to make sure your thirtieth birthday has the happiest ending you could ever dream of."

With a relieved grin, I take the steps two at a time to chase after them, pinning Luck against the door to my studio to kiss them senseless. The second our lips touch, my existence is consumed. I fumble with the key, unwilling to tear away from the plush lips and silken tongue igniting every part of me.

When the lock finally turns, we fall through the door, laughing together. Luck's blazer is the first article of clothing to drop to the floor, followed by my shirt that Luck tears off me, buttons popping off and out of sight. The sight of their curves accentuated with red lace makes my breath catch, and the burn of their hand against my chest, my abs, my hips pulls a soft moan from me. I caress their chest with reverence, first with my hands, then my mouth. Each lap and pinch of their dark nipples through the lace draws a whimper from Luck, as their nails dig into the bare skin of my shoulders.

Their boots and pants follow, Luck kicking everything but their lingerie off as I grip their lush ass and kiss every inch of skin I can reach. The thick wool of their slacks cushions my knees hitting the hardwood moments later. Pinning their hips against the door with a hand splayed across their soft belly, I look up, fighting to catch my breath.

Luck stares down at me, brown eyes wide as they cup my cheek. It takes everything in me to wait for permission, but I lean into their touch, kiss the inside of their wrist, instead of diving frantically between their legs. Every muscle of mine trembles in anticipation as I murmur, "Once I finally get a taste, Luck, I won't want to stop."

With a hard swallow, Luck shudders, their lips parting. At their husky "Please," I hook my thumb under the scrap of red lace to pull it aside, just far enough to bury my face in their cunt. With a moan, I lap at the sweet musk between their thighs like ambrosia.

Luck cries out my name, and their tight grip pulls my hair. Blinking as my eyes roll back from the tug of glorious pain, I force myself to look at them, to drink in every detail of their pleasure. I've imagined this moment, what they'd taste like, how they'd sound—everything is better than my fantasies.

They are dripping over my face, soaking my mustache and beard. I want to drown in them. To commit everything to memory: how they respond to my lips sucking their clit, the arch of their back when I curl my tongue inside them, and how they writhe and babble my name, chanting a quiet demand for more when I replace it with my fingers.

Chest flush, Luck comes with a shudder as their thigh curls tight around my shoulder. I don't slow down, sucking on their clit to keep their pleasure going. My fingers keep stroking steadily until they're gushing over my hand. Luck curls around the arm I have pinning them to the door.

"Felix, that's so much!" Luck manages to gasp between shouted curses, while convulsions wrack through their body. They pull me away by their tight grip on my hair, just far enough to press their foot against my chest; it sends me sprawling onto my back. "Fuck, that's so good. But let a bitch come down a bit, damn!"

With a dazed smile, drunk on the earthy taste of Luck smeared all over my face, I melt under the slight pressure of their foot against my chest. "Sorry."

"No you're not." Luck puts a little more weight onto their foot, pinning me to the floor.

"No, I'm not," I agree, caressing their ankle. "What can I do to make it up to you?"

"Strip," they command, still panting. The softness of their inner thighs is shiny in the dim light, the lace of their panties dark from how soaked I've made them. Luck makes no move to take their foot from my chest as they nod toward my jeans. "My turn to have fun with you."

I scramble to obey, keeping my torso still as I contort myself to pull off my shoes, jeans and boxers. Thank God I spent all week cleaning; the hardwood floors are cold against my bare ass. My dick does not care, aching in anticipation between my thighs for whatever Luck might have in store for me.

"Hands to ankles, cariño," Luck murmurs, and I snap to obey, winding a leg beneath the muscular calf and slender ankle still pinning me to the floor. Luck's bare toes, scarred and strong, graceful yet disfigured after years of ballet with instructors who valued tradition over comfort, look glorious as they press against my sternum. I pull my legs open, a knee on either side of that skillful foot, feeling utterly at their mercy and delighted to be here. "Higher," Luck smirks. "Let me see that hole dripping for me."

"I always imagined you'd be more vanilla," I tease, pulling my ankles back until my knees are around my ears, lower back lifting off the floor. Everything is exposed to their assessing gaze over their shoulder. "But I also imagined this in a bed, at least the first time."

"Oh, is this okay?" Luck asks, the slightest hesitation in their tone.

"Oh fuck, yes!" I sigh, pulling my ankles farther apart. "I'm yours, Luck. Use me."

Their smirk widens. "I knew you'd be a good boy for me, Felix."

A whimper escapes me, and I struggle to breathe, contorting myself impossibly far for them. Cool air whispers against my aching dick, the desire leaking from my front hole.

Disappointment wars with anticipation when Luck finally removes their foot from my chest to walk a slow circle around me. I want to ask what they think, if they're happy with the body I have now. Years of testosterone have given me enough bottom growth that I no longer hate touching myself. The glint in Luck's eye tells me they want to touch me too, and my muscles tremble with need. Content to wait here, bent in half for as long as they want me to be, I lick my lips, moaning at the taste of Luck still clinging to them.

"What do you like?" Luck looks over their shoulder as they tug their thong down their voluptuous hips, cupping their ass with a knowing smirk when they see how enraptured I am by the sight of it. Who could blame me? I want to leave bite marks over every inch, worship their hole with my tongue, tease their clit with my calloused fingers, fill their cunt with my fist. "Any limits I should know?"

"I meant it, Luck." My voice is husky, deep, and I love the way they shiver in response to it. "Whatever you want to do with me, anything, I'm yours."

"If you insist." With one foot on either side of my hips, they wad the red lace up in one hand and dip into a grand plié before me. Because Luck can't squat or kneel like anyone else might. No, they have to *dance* while shoving their panties in my mouth. "Let go of your ankles if you need to stop," Luck murmurs, waiting for my nod before eying my dick and holes, spread wide for them to do whatever they want.

I expect their mouth on me, or perhaps their fingers first. Instead, a glob of spit drops from Luck's smirk, landing directly on my dick. Their thumbs spread it up and down and around the head as they explore me. I moan helplessly, in both pain and pleasure, when they pinch their thumbs together on either side of my shaft. I can only curse through the lace in my mouth, when their fingers slide into my front hole and curl deep inside.

When they lean forward, I lean up to be closer to them, expecting a kiss. Instead, Luck drags their tongue along my lips, adjusting their plié to press their cunt against my dick. I sob at the heat soaking me. The glide of their clit against me. How their pussy squeezes around my dick. The murmur of "Fuck, you taste like me, cariño. You made me come so hard," in my ear.

Luck presses me further into the floor, propping up my lower back with their heels to rock our hips together. I am a helpless mess beneath them, growling curses around the panties stuffed in my mouth, fingers gripping my ankles so tight, I might bruise.

They smirk as they roll their hips, teasing my dick with their cunt. The pleasure mounts higher and higher, until I'm thrashing under them, losing my grip on my ankles from the force of the orgasm tearing through me. Knocked off-balance, Luck lands on their ass with a yelp.

"Oh, fuck, are you okay?" Luck asks, eyes wide in panic as they scramble to their knees to pull the panties from my mouth. The concern lacing their voice irrationally infuriates me. "I thought you were into that—"

"Okay?" I snarl, looping an arm around their hips, hauling them around until their chest is pinned against the foot of the bed a few feet away. Luck muffles a surprised laugh. Behind them, I wedge their knees apart with mine, the fibers from the rug sharp against my skin. "You thought you could ride me like that," I bite the crux of their neck, and Luck sighs out a giggle. "Act so sweet and concerned, like you didn't just degrade me like the filth I am—"

"You're not filth!" Luck protests, but I suck their earlobe until they're moaning instead.

"And you thought a world exists where I would be okay without immediately fucking you senseless the second I came?" I shove a hand between us, roughly pushing two fingers deep into their cunt, milking their soft walls with each thrust of my hips against their ass.

My strap is somewhere, but I just cleaned, and I can't remember where I might have put it. My hand will have to do.

"Fuck, Felix, please!" Luck begs, rolling their hips to take my fingers deeper. I add a third to reward them, and their cunt eagerly stretches to take it. Their hands are fists against the comforter. Luck tosses their curls over their shoulder to look at me, tears in their eyes and my name a prayer on their lips.

I have never resented being short more than right now, but I still stretch forward enough to kiss them. I lose some momentum, but it's worth every second of their tongue against mine, the sweetness of their whimper when my pinkie sinks in to join the rest of my fingers in their heat.

"You are so lucky," I murmur, adjusting my stance to rut my dick against their ass in time with my fingers thrusting slowly into them. "That I remembered you will be showing your ass to the whole town tomorrow night, because I want to mark every inch of you. I want to worship this ass, your fucking tits, your whole glorious body, so everyone can see how much I-" I catch myself, finishing with a stuttered, "How hard I want you."

"Do it," Luck begs. "Bite me, cariño. All over. I want everyone to see you're mine."

"After tomorrow," I promise, rotating my fingers to stretch them open further; a flood leaks from them. "For tonight, this is just for you and me." I carefully push until their cunt swallows my knuckles, my thumb, until my whole hand is deep inside them.

Luck cries out, back bowing as they babble and beg for more in needy whimpers that test my self-control. "You are going to feel me until I get the chance to fuck you properly, 'til I can suck your tits 'til they're bruised, and leave bite marks all over your ass."

With a sob of pleasure, Luck arches their back as I rotate my fist. The knuckle of my thumb presses circles against their front walls. Each roll of their hips pushes their ass into my still-sensitive dick, and I shudder as a second orgasm takes me by surprise. Pressing kisses between their shoulders, I murmur praise—how good they feel around my fist, how well they're taking it, how incredibly hot they are when they're crying from pleasure—and slide my other hand down their stomach to circle their clit.

Within seconds, the silken heat pulses painfully tight around my hand, and Luck muffles their scream into the comforter. I pause, keeping my hand on their clit, but giving them a chance to come down.

Luck shakes their head and murmurs for me to stop.

Concerned I've pushed them too far, I ease my hand from the muscles still clinging to me. "Are you okay?"

Luck smiles over their shoulder, eyes still teary. "Incredibly overstimulated, in the best way possible. That was..." They fall to their side, leaning back against the bed with a dazed laugh, "Wow."

I sit back on my heels, scooting closer to kiss their cheek. "I wasn't too much for you?"

They shake their head, hand wrapping around my neck to keep our foreheads pressed together. "Was I too hard on you?"

"Never." I lean back on my heels, pulling Luck up with me as I rise.

Luck winces as they stand, working out a cramp in their hip. "Is this what being thirty is like? Do I need to stretch after fucking now?"

Shaking out my aching hand (Luck has a very strong pelvic floor), I snort, gesturing to the tidy sitting area of my apartment. "There's room for all the yoga you need now."

Luck beams as they look around for the first time since we walked in. "You cleaned!"

"Yeah, I did the bare minimum for hosting an overnight guest," I snark, pulling them into my arms. Our chaste kiss is too brief for my taste, but we have all night for more. Our whole lives, hopefully. "Let's get ready for bed? We still have our show tomorrow, after all."

Luck kisses me again, longer than I kissed them. "Yeah, round two in bed sounds good."

I laugh, peppering them with kisses as I lead us to the bathroom. The reality of everything sinks in as we squeeze around each other in my tiny bathroom. Luck smiles at me while removing their makeup, and I smile back, forgetting I'm brushing my teeth until Luck is laughing at the toothpaste that splatters my chest.

I've wanted them for years, lusted after them far more than a friend ever should. But all this time, this is what I've wanted: just us, laughing over mundane shit. Content and satiated and comfortable and still wanting more. I can't believe it took a snowstorm and a burlesque show for us to bridge the distance time had created between us, but our performance tomorrow is one I will always cherish.

Sixteen

Luck

The bright light flooding the apartment when I open my eyes tells me it's almost noon. Felix is still snoring next to me, sprawled out and hogging the bed—one hand around my waist and his leg hooked around mine, as if he's afraid I'll leave before he wakes.

I smile as Felix snorts in his sleep. The four days of space that Felix gave me was just enough for me to talk myself out of this a few times, and back into it once more. Why is it so hard to accept that I deserve this? He was so sweet, so attentive last night. A little bossy, a little rough, but so was I, and we both liked that. My pussy is aching this morning in the best way, and I wish the rest of me did, too. I can't wait for Felix to make good on his promise to make me feel him everywhere.

Our date last night, our night together...it was all so easy, so simple, so natural that it was like breathing.

So why does it feel like the other shoe is about to drop? I curl up under Felix's outstretched arm, burying my face in his chest, inhaling the addicting, musky smell of him that gets stronger when he sleeps. The muscles of his waist flex under my hand as he grumbles awake.

"Good morning," Felix murmurs, pressing a kiss to my forehead, to my cheek, to my lips. My heart flutters in my chest. This is just like the other night I stayed here.

This time, I don't give him the chance to hesitate, or myself the opportunity to pull away. I reach up, tugging him down to kiss him properly. Our morning breath is atrocious, but neither of us seem to care, exchanging sweet kisses and caresses. Unhurried affection, as if we have all the time in the world and nowhere to be for hours.

To my dismay, Felix's phone vibrates on the nightstand. The world outside this bed still exists. He ignores it to kiss me more, hand sliding down to massage my ass.

Maybe I can convince him to leave just one bite mark there, as a treat.

But then *my* phone rings, and the ringtone I set for Jorge cuts through the quiet. If it was anyone but one of my brothers calling, I'd ignore it. But Jorge wouldn't be calling me without good reason.

I reach over Felix to find my phone on the nightstand, smiling as Felix wraps his arms around me to kiss my neck.

Before I can say hello, Jorge blurts out, "Paul's here."

My heart drops. "What? Why is Paul there?"

"What?" Felix growls, bolting upright to jump out of bed. I'm left kneeling awkwardly where he was laying beneath me a split second before. Panic clouding my mind, I sit back on my heels.

"For the car, or the money, or his shit back." Jorge's voice is high-pitched, the way it gets when he's anxious. Olive is barking in the background, and a high pitched beep sounds, as if a tow truck is backing up. "He says it's been two weeks."

"But the show is tonight!" My stomach churns at the fearful waver in his voice. Like a stone crashing through thin ice on the lake, the reality sinks in that I might lose my dad's car anyway.

"Nisha won't have the money to pay anything until the bank clears the ticket sales on Monday."

"Luck, what do I do?" Jorge hasn't sounded so young, so afraid since we were kids.

"Here." Felix is already dressed in jeans and his flannel, tossing his Sexy Santas sweatshirt and a pair of joggers to me.

"Just, stall for time, Jorge. I'm on my way." I pull the clothes on, rushing out the door. My boots are cement bricks as I run down the stairs and into the street. Some folks wave at me as I push past them in my rush to get home, but I don't dare slow down, not even to say hi.

Within moments, Felix's truck rumbles up beside me. "Get in!" he calls from the open window.

"No!" I shake my head, pressing toward home as fast as I can. I should have rode Bertha to meet Felix, instead of walking with him last night. I should have known something would go wrong. Getting in a car now would only bring worse luck.

"Luck, get in the damn truck!" Felix pleads.

"I can't risk it!"

"Risk what?" He groans in exasperation. "Being transported somewhere faster than walking?"

"Something bad happening!" I yell, my jaw tight. I know I sound insane, but so what? The situation is already bad. I can't afford to make it worse.

I've been so careful. We didn't walk under the marquee last night. There's been no spilled salt to toss over my shoulder, or broken mirrors to be wary of, not even when one of the tap kids tripped and smacked into it headfirst. No broom has swept my feet. There's no one to put the mal de ojo upon me, because I do my best to uplift everyone around me higher than myself, brighten everyone's day, stay on everyone's good side! Even Paul's!

"Why is this happening?" I whisper.

Giving up with another exasperated groan, Felix tears off down the road towards my house, leaving me stomping after him.

"What can I do, once I get there, anyway?" I ask my boots, instead of begging for them to run with me. Paul will take my dad's car, just like he's taken everything else. All of my parent's savings, the car collection, aside from what was already registered to our names, even my mom's jewelry, all his now. Titi Lydia will let him take my Dancer too, for the sake of keeping the peace in her marriage.

And I will let her husband get away with taking advantage of her softhearted nature, because she's our only family left. Our godmother, who my parents trusted to take care of us, not knowing the depths of her husband's greed.

I shake my head, pushing past the pessimism, and keep walking.

By the time I make it home, there's already a shouting match in the driveway. Jorge is holding back Felix, who is yelling at a smug Paul. Instead of hiding, Olive is barking inside the house, knocking over all of Mom's Christmas decor in the bay window in her attempt to reach Jorge.

When I pass, Felix's truck is still running, door wide open and parked in the street to block the tow truck parked in the driveway.

Burl Cane stands at the end of the driveway, next to his tow truck, looking torn about the argument in front of the garage. He winces in place of a smile when he greets me. "Heya, Luck!"

I'm relieved to see the garage is still closed, that the Eldorado isn't hooked up to be pulled away. "Hi Burl." This isn't his fault, but I can't help but feel betrayed by the sweet man who takes extra care clearing the bike lanes for me.

"Your uncle tells me you're giving him your car?" he asks quietly, before anyone's noticed me.

I shake my head as I stomp past him. "Not if I can help it!"

"We said two weeks!" Felix argues.

"Exactly!" Paul spread his hands, as if he's a bystander caught up in the situation too, instead of the one causing it. "Two weeks ago, we said two weeks. I'm here to collect—" He looks behind his shoulder after Felix and Jorge go still. "Ah, Luck. Good, someone reasonable to talk to."

"I never made any deal with you," I snap. "You can't have it!"

"So I'll just have your boyfriend here arrested for theft then?" Paul crosses his arms. "Tell everyone in Sleighbell Springs that Ho Ho Handyman is letting a lowlife cut corners on all of the work they do around town?" His lip curls into a sneer. "Oh, funnily enough, the Chamber of Holiday Cheer just received a new business application, for Krampus Construction? A bit mean-spirited of a name, in my opinion. I'm sure the rest of the Chamber would agree with me." Paul chuckles, "They always do."

"Go right ahead, you piece of shit!" Felix barks. "Let's see who believes you!"

Paul raises an eyebrow. "Or perhaps since your brother agreed to give me a car if I didn't get my property back by today, I can take his Firebird instead."

"No!" I blurt out. Jorge's car is his most cherished possession; restoring it helped him heal from the accident. And Felix's dad is already in enough trouble with his business; Felix has been worried about Ho Ho Handyman failing for years. I can't risk either of them losing anything. Especially not if Felix is finally starting his own company.

"No?" Paul smirks at me. "So you can just go ahead and open the garage, let our friend Burl here tow what's mine back to my house, and I'll forget and forgive all this nasty business." Paul makes it sound like the most reasonable suggestion, when the very idea would split my heart in two.

"Give us 'til tomorrow!" I plead, blocking Felix and Jorge behind me. This is my car, my uncle, my favor that I asked of Felix. This is my fight. "The show is tonight, and it's sold out, so we're good for the money come Monday, but I promise, we'll bring you the materials back tomorrow, first thing in the morning. We just need to keep the theater open for tonight."

"You might have to do what Luck says, Paul," Burl interrupts. "If Luck doesn't give permission for me to take their property, I would need a court order to remove it."

Paul scoffs, his face clouding. "If I don't have my property back by *midnight*, I am suing. All three of you, and the theater! I'll get what's due to me, one way or another. Verbal agreements are enforceable in Vermont, and my wife witnessed the whole conversation." Not even bothering to look at me, he sneers at Felix, "All of my materials back, in my shed where they belong, before the end of the day. Got it? Or all that money you're raising will go to my lawyer, in the end. It'll be in *all* of your best interests to cooperate."

I manage to keep it together until Paul's SUV disappears around the corner. My eyes burn from the hollow ache in my chest, and I do my best to blink back the tears before Felix and my brother can see.

"Luck," Felix murmurs from behind me, so gentle it's infuriating. My jaw tightens when his hand, hesitant and kind, touches my shoulder.

Jorge groans. "I'm so sorry, Lucky, I never thought he'd be such an—"

"No." I shake my head, tears welling in my eyes in spite of my efforts. "You knew. We've all known what kind of man he is. And you agreed anyway. Both of you did."

Felix's face is stricken when I turn around to shake his hand from my shoulder, Jorge's downcast.

"I hate him," I whisper, holding my brother's eyes when he looks up in surprise. "I hate that *he's* what we're stuck with, that Mom and Dad aren't here to put him in his place. I hate that he gets away with walking all over us, even now that we're grown." My gaze flicks to Felix. "I hate that this was your only choice, and you were forced to make it for me, that I asked you to help Nisha and Twyla. I should have known-" My voice breaks. "I should have known this would happen. This was a mistake." A tear rolls down my cheek, and Felix shakes his head. "I just wanted to help."

Before I can lose it completely, I turn on my heel, and run down the driveway, scrambling into the open door of Felix's truck. I haven't driven a car in nine years, three months, and two days. But shifting the gear into drive and pressing the accelerator is the easiest thing in the world.

Seventeen

Felix

Luck is halfway down the block when it sinks in that they just stole my truck. Luck, who hasn't driven since they were twenty-one. Who has panic attacks at the very idea of getting into a car. Who has biked through countless blizzards and heat waves and thunderstorms on the wafer-thin excuse that it's good for the environment, their health, and they just really really like biking.

Concern tightens in my chest, replacing the burning rage I've been unleashing on Paul for the ten minutes before Luck stomped up the driveway. "We have to go after them."

At my first step towards the garage, Jorge tightens his grip around my chest, pulling me back against him. "Nope."

"But they're gonna have a panic attack—"

"Still nope."

"What happens if they get in an accident?" I blurt out. Visions of every fear Luck has confided in me over the past decade are racing through my mind.

"Felix, Luck left because they're upset. And you know as well as I do that they need space when they're upset." Jorge's arm around my chest is joined by his other one, wrapping me in a grounding hug. "They know how to drive, our dad made sure of it. If they get stuck and can't get back, they'll call us and we'll go get them. Or bring Bertha to them, whatever they need."

"What do I do?" My voice rasps. "They said this was a mistake. I can't let them leave thinking we're a mistake." Luck's words echo in my mind, the resentment in their voice a poison curling through my veins.

Jorge sighs. "If they were talking about you—and I highly doubt they were—then you have a conversation about it when they're ready. You know Luck, Felix. You know them better than anyone, even me. If you go after them now, their stubborn ass will double down and shut you out. They'll pretend nothing is wrong and pull away to protect themself. Even if they didn't mean that your date last night was a mistake, if you go after them now and push them for validation, you'll end up making it about you and your date, instead of whatever Luck needs to process."

My throat tightens. "You and your fucking therapy, man."

Jorge snorts, patting my chest.

"I just..." I shake my head, chest aching. "No job or fucking scrap metal is worth Luck's connection to your dad, and it's not worth losing them. I love them, so much. I always have, and I'll never forgive myself if I fucked everything up by agreeing to Paul's fucking scam."

"We'll figure it out," Jorge says simply, letting me go, but keeping a grip on my elbow. His brown eyes, so much like Luck's, are soft and sympathetic. Wise, as always, beyond his years. "Of course you love them, everyone knows it, even Luck. But Luck isn't in the right space to hear that right now."

"I know." My heart aches at the idea of staying here when Luck is upset, but Jorge is right. "Chasing after them just to tell them that won't fix anything."

"So what can you do instead?" Jorge prompts. "What does Luck need from you now?"

My jaw works back and forth for a long moment. "The show."

Jorge nods. "The show."

"What if they're not back in time for—" I start to ask, already knowing the answer Luck would give me. "The show must go on."

Jorge nods again. "And you know *I* don't know shit about dancing, so it's gotta be you."

"I haven't produced a show—" I huff, cutting my self-defeating talk as Burl Cane starts awkwardly walking along his truck in our direction.

Burl takes off his trapper hat, running his hand over his thinning hair, before putting the buffalo print hat back on. "Look, this is awkward business with Paul, but you have my word I'm not taking that car unless the sheriff makes me, okay? I don't want nothing to do with any shady business, and I don't like all that stuff Paul was saying, with the blacklisting your dad's company and everything." He winces awkwardly, like his son Aiden does whenever he messes up a dance move. "Joe Kelly may not be very good with money, but he's a damn good handyman, and a good honest guy. And so are you, and your brother. If it comes down to it, you'll always have me at your back. The whole town, because that kind of deal isn't what Sleighbell Springs is about."

"Thanks, Burl." While his support is an empty promise, if Paul follows through with suing us (all three of us *and* the Sleighbell Stage, for some reason), I still appreciate the gesture. At least the town has our backs; even if Paul is influential in the Chamber of Holiday Cheer, he can't take on everyone in Sleighbell Springs. Luck is too well-loved for everyone to stand by and let Paul get away with this. Nisha and Twyla have brought too much energy and positivity into town for anyone to let the Sleighbell Stage close; why else would the show be sold out?

Still, the courts might not agree, and legal fees would eat any cushion we might raise tonight. I have to do everything I can to make this show the best damn performance Sleighbell Springs has ever seen. And keep Luck's Eldorado in their garage for as long as they need it to be, until they're ready to do something with it.

I turn to Jorge. "Can you drive me? I got a few stops to make."

With a knowing smirk, Jorge nods. "I knew you would."

Eighteen

Luck

I DRIVE WITHOUT KNOWING where I'm going, with no awareness of how long it's been other than realizing how far I was from home when I turned back south at the Canadian border. Every turn is instinctual. Each time I fiddle with the fan or adjust the mirrors is like breathing, like it hasn't been almost ten years since I've driven. My only companions are the mountains and the lake, the forest around Sleighbell Springs, and the rock music on Felix's favorite station.

As the sunlight blazes orange and red across the sky, dark clouds soaring high overhead, I find myself at the wrought iron gates of the Sleighbell Springs cemetery. They open automatically as I approach, inviting me in to slowly crawl along the winding paths among the headstones and monuments.

I turn off the engine just as a roll of thunder rumbles through, and a cold spring rain patters against the windshield. Climbing down from the truck, I walk to where my parents are laid to rest.

I haven't been back here since their funeral. That day was the first time I walked home, instead of driving. I had a panic attack about a block from the funeral home. All three of my brothers in the car with me witnessed how broken I'd become; they tried to comfort me in the driver's seat as we pulled off on the side of the road.

Thursday Holiday, the funeral home director's then-teenage son, had ended up calming me down enough to drive me in the hearse carrying my mother. His mother helped a still-injured Jorge into the front passenger seat of the hearse carrying our father. My aunt and uncle drove my younger brothers, with Jorge's wheelchair in the trunk. Thursday was just helping his mom out with driving the second hearse, barely old enough to have his license in the first place, and the poor kid got saddled with me having a breakdown in his passenger seat. But Thursday was exactly what I needed then: quiet, supportive, and caring.

It was not my first panic attack, nor my last, but it was one that shook me past the point of logic. Once Thursday and his mom got me together enough to get me through the funeral, escorting my mom felt like an honor, a rite of passage. Without that purpose? Not even Thursday's calm energy could get me back in anyone's car afterward.

The hour walk home, Felix was half a step behind me and silent the whole time. Titi Lydia drove Luis and Efrain home, and the Kellys made Jorge comfortable in their car. The hours of walking home in the cold made my feet ache worse than they ever had in pointe shoes, and the muscles in my thighs twitched for hours after. But as with ballet, that pain was strength, that numbness a reminder that I didn't have to be afraid, because I was powerful and capable and safe with my own two feet.

Rain is sharp and cold on my face as I stand before my parents' headstone, the first of Lydia and Paul's "gifts" that actually came from the estate. Cold seeps through my borrowed sweatpants, and my whole body aches—from panic, from the pleasure of last night, from anger.

"I wish you were here," I whisper. The hot tears that well up join the rain dripping down my cheeks. "How could you leave us like this? Leave me? I never wanted this! I wanted to live my life, travel the world, be the rich, mysterious auntie. Not raising my brothers, especially not without you here." I shake my head. "I love this place, and I'm happy, but I wanted more for myself! Why couldn't I have that?" Burying my face in my hands, I sniffle. "And why do I blame myself for not getting that?"

I fall to my knees, muffling my sob in my hands. "You shouldn't have come to my performance." Another sob wracks my body, because why am I angry that my parents loved me, supported my dreams? "Why couldn't you stay home that night, instead of driving all the fucking way to the city to see me? It was just another recital. You'd seen hundreds of them. So why did I invite you? Why did Jorge have to come with you?"

How long I cry, feeling sorry for myself, missing my parents, regretting how everything turned out, I don't know. Eventually, I run out of tears, and my shaking is more from the cold rain than grief.

When my whole body is sore and aching and spent, I shake my head. "It wasn't my fault." My voice is hoarse, and I clear it, speaking louder this time. "How can I regret it, when I didn't do anything wrong?"

It was an accident. It was a snowstorm. It was just plain bad luck.

Even if it took me nine years to be ready to accept it, their death wasn't my fault. As if in penance for a sin I never committed, I gave up my life, gave up my dreams, gave up everything but dance. After it happened, I did everything I could for my family, my brothers. I doubt I could have handled any of it if it weren't for Felix. He's always been there for me for the past twelve years, no matter how much I've kept him at arm's length. Just half a step behind, ready to support me, ready to listen, ready to do whatever I needed from him.

"It wasn't a mistake." The tears roll anew, welling from some untapped grief I haven't unpacked yet. My knees are numb where they're buried in slush. Ice cold rain and snow soaks into my skin through the Sexy Santas sweatshirt Felix threw at me this morning. Felix wasn't a mistake. This show wasn't a mistake. None of it was. But the stricken hurt on Felix's face is all I can think of.

"What am I doing here?" I blink, a rush of awareness and panic hitting me all at once. Horror sinks in at the realization of how he must have taken my panicked, disconnected thoughts. How I left him after saying this was a mistake, right before our— "Oh my god, the show!" I jump to my feet, taking in where I am, how I got here, how fucking late I must be.

Felix's truck waits for me, but my feet won't lead me to it, no matter how hard I beg them to just get in the cab again.

I'm stuck, with no way of getting back. Thinking about driving in the freezing rain makes my throat tighten in fear all over again, and I choke out a sob.

I should already be at the theater. I should be sweet-talking whoever's working at the hardware store tonight to make a late-night delivery. I should be giving a pep talk to my class, surrounded by my dance community, with Felix.

Instead, I am here, crying over my parents grave, who passed almost a decade ago, and the boy whose heart I broke the second he gave it to me. I'm over an hour's walk from town, shivering from the freezing rain pelting me, and I haven't eaten or drank anything today.

"What was I thinking?" Helplessness bleeds into the panic that wracks my chest. "Fuck, I wasn't thinking! I'm never thinking!"

The automated gate clicks as it swings open, and a familiar hearse pulls into the graveyard. The black Cadillac creeps along slowly down the path, going the five-mile-an-hour speed limit that I certainly didn't follow, until it finally parks behind Felix's truck.

The door opens, and a familiar head of auburn hair, followed by an umbrella, pops up. Thursday Holiday squints at me from under the black edges of the umbrella. "Luck, is that you? Isn't your show tonight?"

Relief floods me. "Thursday, can you give me a ride? I have a few stops to make."

Nineteen

Felix

"Any sign of Luck?" Estelle asks me for the eighth time as she wrings her hands. Nisha just called ten minutes to curtain. Everyone is dressed, warmed up, and as ready as they can be without their teacher and the producer of this show. The crowd in the theater buzzes with conversation and laughter.

Thumbs tucked into my tool belt to give my hands something to do, I shake my head, my jaw tight. "Not yet."

I should have gone after Luck.

"What do we do?" Junie asks, staring at the setlist on her clipboard. "They're in the opening number after you and May do the intro. Do we just skip it until they show up?"

"Let me see that." I frown as I read over it. Luck laid it out so that each act opened with a group number for everyone in the class, then worked their solo or group acts in between the other performers—the drag queens, the pole dancers, and the aerialists.

I reach for the pencil I always keep in my tool belt, but my hand comes away empty; I'm only wearing it to take off in a few minutes. "Anyone got a pen?"

Estelle digs through her purse tucked backstage, to hand me a glittery pink gel pen. It'll have to do.

"Everyone, listen up—here's what we're gonna do!" I prop my knee up on a chair as the group gathers around me. Adjusting her giant and perfectly coiffed wig, May smiles at me when I catch her eye in the back; normally I defer to her in everything at Sleigh Queen, because she's the boss. But this is Luck's show, and if they're not here to make it happen, I will. "We're making a change to the order, to give Luck more time to get here. May and I are still going first, then it's the Backstreet Boys—"

"We're going first?" Avery squeaks, their eyes wide as usual.

"Yup!" I nod, trying to reassure them silently that they have nothing to fear. "Our rehearsals have been solid. We're ready. All of us."

Still trepidacious, Avery nods. The ever-skeptical Keiran asks, "How are you going to change that fast?"

I'll change as fast as I need to, is what my inner jackass wants to say. But I'm filling Luck's shoes right now. Instead, I ask, "May, you can buy me time for a quick change, right?"

"You know I can, darling!" May winks.

I list the rest of the acts, trying to get Luck enough time to get here in the first act. "Second to last is WAP, and then I Am What I Am to close out the first half."

"Oh, you're making me emcee the second half after *that*?" May tsks. "I'll be naked. Literally and metaphorically! Luck said I could go at the end!"

I level a look at my boss and drag mother. "May, I've seen you get in full face in five minutes flat."

"Yeah, but it's not good!" May pouts. "Fine, but you need to emcee if I'm not ready yet."

"Done," I nod. I loathe public speaking, but I'll do whatever it takes, even stammering into a mic for a few minutes. Hopefully, Luck will be here by then. If they aren't in a ditch somewhere, or stuck in the middle of nowhere, because they're afraid to get back in the truck.

Jorge has my phone, if they call me instead of him during the show.

"Wait, who will be the front person in WAP?" Aaron asks. "Luck is supposed to cue us to do solos during the verses."

"Any volunteers?" I ask, looking around. Everyone in the burlesque class avoids my eye. "I guess that leaves me."

"Do you know the choreo?" Junie asks skeptically.

I blink. After three weeks of watching Luck rehearse it, how could I not? Every movement, every pop and lock, every bounce of their hips, every shimmy is ingrained in my memory. "I'll manage." I clear my throat. "And we'll revisit the second act more during intermission, depending on if and when Luck gets there."

Everyone stares at me, waiting.

"What?" I ask. "Did I forget something?"

"Are you gonna give us a pep talk?" Estelle asks, fussing with the bunny ears secured around her puff. "Luck always gives us one before performances."

As much as I'm tempted to retort that I'm not Luck, the pep talk is a key part of their pre-show ritual. Whether they're in charge of the performance or not, they always have an encouraging speech for whoever needs to hear it.

May smiles at me expectantly and nods encouragingly.

I huff, trying to figure out what to say now that everyone is listening intently. Telling the group about the change in plans is much different than giving a pep talk. Even as co-captains back in high school, that was always Luck's job. "I know it might seem weird, or scary, or whatever, that Luck isn't here yet. They're your teacher, the organizer, and it's easy to let their absence get in your head to bring you down." My heart clenches when Avery glances at the floor, when Estelle and Junie exchange a look. "But you're all here tonight to show off your skills, your talent, your passion—"

"And our sexy ass bodies!" Aaron chips in.

With a snort, I nod. "And our sexy ass bodies. We're going to melt the last of winter away from Sleighbell Springs, or whatever Luck said the other day, and give everyone a reason to tip us to help the theater stay open." I look around, encouraged by the nods from Nome and Aiden. "Luck has led you to this point, taught you everything you need to know to go out and rock everyone's socks off." I cringe at how much I sound like Luck, talking in cheesy cliches. It just makes me worry about them all the more.

Everyone looks at me, still waiting expectantly.

"What?" I ask.

"You're supposed to do the hand thing," Estelle explains. "And lead us in a cheer with our team name."

"Really?" I groan, but I put my hand out anyway. Everyone piles in, hands slapping atop another. Even Dove, May, and the other performers not in the class join in. I huff, frowning. "Go...Sexy Santas."

Ignoring my deadpan tone at that corny team name, everyone shouts "Sexy Santas!" at the top of their lungs. A murmur of laughter ripples from the audience.

"Aaron," I catch his elbow before he can scurry away.

"Yeah, babe?" he asks, putting his arm around me.

"Can you bring the updated setlist to the booth?" I squeeze his arm. "Don't let Twyla steal it, just have her copy the changes on her setlist, and bring it back. May needs this to emcee. I don't want any missed cues because we don't know who's next."

Aaron nods, a sympathetic smile on his face. "Luck is going to be okay, Felix."

My throat tightens as the lights flick up and down for everyone to take their seats. I frown. "They better be."

"There's our grumpy bastard." Aaron pats my cheek, skipping off to the booth.

"Ready to get this show on the road with me, darling?" May asks, as kind as always, in her own way. "You okay?"

"Ready." I don't answer her second question, gesturing for her to go out onstage as the house lights go dark and the opening bars of the piano play May's intro number. I'm worried, I'm anxious, I'm regretting following Jorge's advice to go on with the show. I think May must sense that, because she doesn't push the question I avoided.

But this is what Luck would want me to do. What they'd want all of us to do. Because this isn't about me, or Luck, or even their Eldorado. This is about saving the Sleighbell Stage.

As we've rehearsed, I slide out onto the stage on my knees at May's cue. My stage persona of Felix Navidad comes like second nature in May's company, though our audience tonight is much different than Sleigh Queen's usual clientèle. A cocky grin on my face, I play up taking off my tool belt until May is satisfied with the level of cheers coming from the audience. I slowly unbutton my flannel and rebutton it, teasing the green harness I'm wearing underneath, until enough tips have been thrown my direction.

"Now here's why I introduced our lovely Felix Navidad as our bendover boy tonight!" May hooks a finger through my belt loop, and pulls my faux-leather pants away in one fell swoop, leaving me in the tight black shorts I'll be wearing for the rest of the evening.

The audience erupts in cheers, and I shake my ass as I bend over to pick up the dollar bills scattered on the stage. The house lights are too bright to make out any faces, and for that I am grateful, because I can hear my brother's groan from somewhere.

At least my parents didn't come!

"Now, the theme of tonight is the Sleighbell Spring Awakening, to encourage it to stop fucking snowing already!" May banters to the audience. "So you may know Felix here as our head elf in town, but tonight? He's Sleighbell Springs' very own Leprechaun!" May tosses a green top hat in the air. I do my best to catch it with my head, but I miss, because we didn't rehearse that bit. Typical May.

The audience cheers anyway, even more so when I make a show of putting the dollar bills inside before settling it over my hair.

"Bendover boy, don't forget your stripper droppings!" May teases, dropping the pants to the floor behind me.

Tossing the pleather pants I borrowed from Nome over my shoulder along with my flannel and tool belt, I scurry offstage for my quick change into the all-white Millennial look. For the sake of time, I keep my black shorts and green harness on, and dump the bills in the oversized Easter basket we're using to collect tips.

"We ready?" I ask everyone quietly, clapping Avery on the shoulder to jolt the stage fright in their eyes away. They look like they're about to hurl from nerves. "We're setting the energy for the show, so let's have fun and get everyone singing and dancing along with us."

Everyone nods, and even Avery sets their chin in determination. A sense of stubborn serenity settles over us as we line up behind the curtain. As the smoke machines billow around our feet, I feel the anticipation spread to the rest of our crew.

Even if Luck doesn't make it tonight, wherever they are, this is for them, for their friends, for the theater they call home. Whether they know it or not, everyone is here for Luck's sake.

NUMBER AFTER NUMBER, EACH act seamlessly transitions into the next, even when they don't go perfectly. Everyone is professional, none more so than May, who guides the audience through stories and banter whenever there's a delay getting the lyra hoop down, or cracks a joke when Estelle's Easter bunny tail falls off as she's hopping offstage.

We're at the final number of the first half, but Luck is still not here. From the wings, I'm dripping with sweat after winging my way through WAP, and watching May sing her heart out to "I Am What I Am." Slowly pulling away her drag piece by piece—dress, body pads and stockings, wig, and even her makeup—May is stripped away to reveal a vulnerable Mason underneath.

My own heart aches from the evocative mood of her performance, while the room explodes in rapturous applause as the song ends. When I swallow the lump in my throat away, it immediately grows back at the realization that we're at intermission, and I haven't heard from Luck.

Quiet as a ghost, Jorge pops up beside me. "Luck just texted, they're on the way."

"What?" I blurt out, louder than intended. But thankfully the applause is still going, so only those backstage heard me.

I hurry after Jorge, following him out to the front. The cold wind and freezing rain pelt my bare skin, but I can't care. Luck is on their way. They're okay. They're safe.

A lone pair of headlights—not my truck—creeps down Mistletoe Street. My heart clenches when the black vehicle rolls under a streetlight, revealing the long body of a Forever Holiday hearse. Jorge's breath gets more and more rapid as the hearse approaches, and I take his hand.

To our relief, Luck hops out of the passenger side door. "I am so sorry I am late! I hope you started the show without me!"

Both Jorge and I reach for them to hug them, but they run past us, through the doors, hurtling for the door that leads backstage. My gut sinks when Luck doesn't even spare me a passing glance.

Jorge pushes my shoulder. "Go!"

"Right!" I wipe my cold and dirty feet on the plush carpet as I follow Luck, weaving through the lines of people getting a drink from Tucker Envy and Carlyle during intermission, the crowd browsing the silent auction, and past the gourmet concessions and red carpet photoshoot. I catch up to Luck just as they make it backstage. The rest of the cast greets them with a group hug, before I can make sure they're safe.

I hover at the edges as everyone fills Luck in on what they missed, asks them where the hell they've been, and if they're okay.

Luck gives me a tentative smile when they see their outfits hanging up, their makeup bag and collection of pasties waiting for them on a dressing table. I want to hold them, kiss them, beg them for forgiveness. For assuming Paul would be a decent person, instead of a complete scumbag.

But Luck looks away, busies themself with getting ready for the group number at the start of the second act, asking Estelle and Junie and everyone else how their numbers went, laughing brightly when Aaron gives them a play by play of how well I took over their role for the WAP choreo, considering I've never once rehearsed it. Avery chatters excitedly over him, about how they went almost Full Monty and loved every second!

To anyone else, Luck seems fine. Excited even, and cheerful, if frazzled. Vague about where they were, what took them so long to get there.

However, I have known Luck for twenty-five years, and they are barely keeping it together. Anxiety ripples from their fumbling movements as they do their makeup, stubbornness in their too-bright laugh.

I want to comfort them, but I don't know if Luck wants me to. If they'd let me, or if it would push them away more. "This was a mistake" echoes through my head, my heart, the way it has all evening.

Luck may not be ready for me yet, but I've been waiting a long time. It aches to keep my distance, to give them the space they need, but I can wait until they're ready. After all, I'm not going anywhere, and I am certainly not giving up.

Twenty

Luck

My makeup is awful, but it's on my face. My hair? A mess, but done securely enough that my headpieces for the numbers I have left can be pinned into place within seconds. My gnarly toes, still freezing but as warmed up as they can be in ten minutes, wiggle in my dance heels. I hope I don't cramp, especially after scarfing down the fast food Thursday bought for me on the way. But if I do, the show must go on, and I did this to myself.

At the makeup station next to me, May is still reapplying her face. "Luck, babe, can you emcee the first number? Felix said he'd cover for me, but I can't imagine how good he'd be at crowdwork. He'd probably cuss everyone out for not donating more."

"I'm right here, May," Felix grumbles.

I jump at how close he is, lurking by the door of the greenroom.

"And am I wrong, darling?" May purses her lips as she frantically rouges her cheeks.

Felix snorts. "No."

"Exactly," May deadpans, then bats her eyelashes at me. "Luck, you got me?"

"What do I say?" I ask.

"You'll figure it out." May shrugs, brushing powder from the carefully blended contour of her cleavage. "Since this is a group number, just introduce the class, talk more about the fundraiser after the dance, and I'll take over after the second song."

"Thanks, May." A pre-show pep talk is one thing; I have no idea how to emcee a performance. Felix catches my arm as I pass through the door. My heart is in my throat at how warm his hand is against my chilled skin, even through the silk of the opera gloves I'll be pulling off onstage.

I look into his blue eyes, waiting for him to say something, anything. He must be furious with me. For taking off like that, for not calling him, for stealing his truck. For making him think our night together was a mistake.

His jaw tightens, and he finally mutters, "You'll need this." Felix holds out the microphone, pulling his hand away as soon as I grasp it, before my fingers can brush his.

"Thanks." I push past him just as the lights flick up and down, signaling the end of intermission.

The stage lights blind me for a few seconds until I blink past them. Everyone in Sleighbell Springs has turned out for this. My brother and Rudy sit next to each other in the back, Olive in her own seat between them. Thursday has found an empty seat next to Burl, Cindy, and the rest of the Cane family. The crew from Sleigh Queen, Miles Dalton in tow, has claimed the front row, and an embarrassing number of my younger students' parents are in the audience.

Everyone cheers as I walk across the stage. My feet automatically settle into a cha-cha to the nonexistent beat, with a smile on my face.

"Good evening, Sleighbell Springs!" The mic squeals with feedback, but I wince along with everyone until I've found a safe spot to stand. "Welcome to the second half of the first ever Sleighbell Spring Awakening burlesque show!"

While I wait for the applause to die down, I settle into a comfortable, yet confident showgirl stance. "As I'm sure all of you know, I'm Luck, the owner and teacher at Dancers and Prancers, a business my brothers and I inherited from our late parents, who passed just over nine years ago."

The crowd nods sympathetically.

"While I'm sure they never imagined I'd turn their treasured showroom into a space that cultivates stripping and debauchery..." The crowd chuckles along with me. "I know they'd be proud of me, and all of my brothers, for building on their legacy in our own ways. So believe me when I say I'm so appreciative of each and every one of you for coming out to support our inaugural burlesque class here in Sleighbell Springs. We've all worked so hard, and learned so much over the past few months, and each and every one of these Sexy Santas has made me so proud!"

The crowd cheers, my brother's piercing whistle cutting through the applause.

I nod to Twyla and Nisha in the control room, and the first bars of "Titi Me Pregunto" play. "Please put your hands together to welcome to the stage, the Sexy Santas!"

As the room cheers, Estelle and Junie lead a line of students each from either side of the stage, cha-chaing their way to the beat, just like I had. I call out their names into the mic, one by one, giving them a moment to do a solo and hyping them up with the rest of the class. During each chorus, we all collectively remove our gloves—or stockings or shorts or whatever clothing we're wearing. Once we reach the final bars of the song, we strike our final poses together, the way we've rehearsed week after week, as naked as we can legally be.

The smiles on everyone's faces at the bills raining on the stage and the cheers from the crowd are infectious. Any lingering guilt and dread and exhaustion is muffled by my pride and joy in these lovely people, who have trusted me to bring them together like this. Everyone piles into a group hug around me onstage, as if the class somehow senses I need a moment with them—a silent, affectionate, sweaty *thank you for going on with the show, for your trust, for everything*. My face somehow gets wedged into Aaron's armpit, but I can't be bothered to care.

Felix rushes out as the applause dies down, exaggerating his grumpiness at how many stripper droppings he has to pick up. It's a bit we planned for the first half, and I'm relieved he saved it for me, now that our song will be the finale of the show. Hands on his hips, Felix disappears backstage in a huff, only to bring out a laundry basket, making the crowd laugh. As all of the performers scurry offstage to help with quick changes and bring down the aerial silks for the next performance, he bends over to pick up the tips.

"You might be wondering what we're raising money for!" I tear my eyes away from his tight little ass, exposed for the whole town to see. The surge of jealousy is accompanied by a single thought, a primal rush of *mine* that can't be healthy. I do my best to smother it as I beam out at the audience; the urge to casually touch him, rest my hand on his ass and stake my claim, persists. "As I'm sure May told you in the first half, our beloved institution in town, the Sleighbell Stage, experienced some significant storm damage a few weeks ago. This historical theater has hosted countless *Nutcracker* performances, concerts from touring musicians, comedy acts, and I would bet a lot of money that most of us walked across this stage for our high school graduations!"

The crowd chuckles.

"Exactly!" I grin. "Any and all tips, purchases, silent auction bids, and ticket sales are benefiting the building fund, to keep the Sleighbell Stage thriving for future generations to enjoy Christmas cheer!" May was right, the words keep coming naturally to me. But then I remember the bit Felix and I have planned. Hopefully he doesn't mind a bit of improv.

As I'd hoped, he's standing just behind me, waiting. At my glance, Felix rushes forward, shoving a wad of money at me.

"Is this what we raised in this number?" I ask.

Felix nods, but when I reach for it, he pulls it just out of reach.

"Felix..." I warn.

He holds out one dollar, letting me take it from his hand.

The next he tucks into his harness, puffing out that chest of his as he smirks. The audience cheers.

As I yank it out of his harness, I frown, as we rehearsed, wishing I could flirt back instead. "Felix, stop playing games!"

Felix pouts, encouraging the audience to "aww" in sympathy, but I wonder how much of his dejection is real. I should have come back sooner, given us a chance to talk things out, before we rushed right onstage.

Still improvising on the bit we had planned for the first act, Felix puts a bill between his lips, puckering up. He dodges my hand when I reach for it, instead silently encouraging me to take it from him with my own mouth. The audience cheers wildly for me to kiss him.

God, I want to, and then kiss him over and over again until he can feel how sorry I am that I ran like that.

But no, that's not what we planned.

Instead, I play up the annoyance and grab him by the throat. I'm supposed to take the bill from his mouth, push him away, and pretend to be annoyed by his flirting.

However, something inside of me keeps my hand around the strong muscles, the pulse fluttering under my thumb. Keeping Felix close, but still at arm's length, just like I have for twelve years. He looks back at me, blue eyes wide.

At the barest prompting from the tension in my hand, Felix kneels, spitting the dollar bill from his mouth back into the wad of cash clenched in his hands. He holds the whole fistful out to me.

"Good boy," I croon into the mic as I pat his head, and the crowd eats that up just as much as the idea of us kissing. Out of the corner of my eye, Estelle gives me the thumbs-up that the silks are ready. "That wasn't so hard, was it? No more games, okay? You be a good bendover boy and put that in the Easter basket where it belongs."

Felix nods, bowing as he backs offstage. The crowd laughs as he scrambles back for the laundry basket full of gloves and dresses.

"Let's keep that same energy, shall we?" I turn back to the audience, my smile trembling from how public that moment was that Felix and I just had. Pride rushes through me, knowing that everyone in town got to see him kneel, for *me*. "Every dollar goes directly toward restoring the damage of the Sleighbell Stage! To encourage your generous financial support, please welcome to the stage Ginger Snap!"

As the heavy beats of "Earned It" by the Weeknd come over the speakers, I slink offstage.

In full face and outfit, May greets me, holding out her hand for the mic.

But when I go to hand it to her, she pulls me into a hug. "That was perfect, my dear."

My cheeks heat as she presses my face into the padding of her cleavage. I've always looked up to May, but she's always been part of Felix's life, not mine. I might be reading way too much into this hug, because for the first time, I feel like I'm a part of the Sleigh Queen family, too. "Thanks, May."

"I never expected Felix would be *quite* that submissive," May teases. "But I always knew you'd be the top in this relationship."

I choke, my fluster scattering any coherence in my protests. Or perhaps I'm unwilling to deny that Felix and I are...something now. If we still are something, anyway.

But Felix is nowhere to be seen. For the next few acts, he always manages to end up across the stage from me. Junie blows everyone out of the water with her cowgirl rendition of Pony, and Aaron and Nome do the most homoerotic chair performance of "Call My By Your Name" I've ever seen. By the time Dove Devlin is onstage, her strong body climbing her pole to "Pour Some Sugar On Me," I'm convinced he's avoiding me on purpose.

Just as May is introducing my solo, Felix appears at my elbow, standing just behind me. "Break a leg," he murmurs into my ear, pressing a quick kiss to my cheek. His body heat radiates across the centimeters between us. The tips of his fingers sear through the red satin corset accentuating my curves, as his soft touch traces down my back.

I don't have a chance to respond; I'm about to miss my cue. Already, a few bars of "You Don't Own Me" have gone by. Instead of leaning back against him, showing him how sorry I am, I step onto the stage, chin held high.

This is the routine I've had memorized since I took my first burlesque class; it's my comfort zone. My way of reclaiming myself, my queerness, my gender fuckery, through the very movements and culture that had trapped me in the first place. This song freed me.

In the spotlight, I pull my glove off with my teeth, finger by finger until the silk slips from my arm. Suddenly, I am twenty again, living in New York and dancing at some amateur night at a cash-only underground club, carefree and naive. Confidence fills my chest as I drop my hips. Teasing my thighs with the glove, I pull it through my legs to the cheers of the audience, rocking my hips to the beat.

I have to trust Felix and I to figure it out. Just like I know this town will take care of their own, newcomers like Nisha and Twyla included. Or how I believe in myself to keep going, for myself and everyone else who counts on me. How I count on Felix, how I've counted on him since we were kids—for everything.

As the song winds to a close, I end my routine with floor work at the edge of the stage, inviting the audience into a closer connection with me. Moving smoothly from a body slide into a pinup pose, I hold my corset aloft with a smirk, teasing the audience with a shimmy of my pasty-covered tits. The crowd erupts, and Olive woos along from the back of the theater.

As part of our bit, Felix slides out onto the stage on his knees (thankfully he's already got the kneepads for our finale on), scrambling to help me up.

An echo of last night, I push him onto his back with my foot and step over him, gesturing for him to pick up the tips instead. May teases us as she comes onstage to work the crowd, while Felix picks everything up. Instead of disappearing backstage to change, I find myself folding my arms over my chest as I sternly make sure he picks up every dollar. It wasn't planned, but I can't bear to leave him behind.

As soon as he's picked up my last glove, I grab the nape of his neck and strong-arm him off the stage. Once again, keeping him at arm's length, but still close. The audience ripples with laughter, louder when May makes a shady quip about Felix once we're offstage.

Without a single word, we part ways, Felix already ready for our number. I disappear into the greenroom to dress, barely making it back in time to catch Estelle's final number—a ballet-infused fan dance to "Pink Pony Club"—as I tuck the last pins securing my feathered rainbow head piece into my hair.

Estelle never removes a single stitch of clothing; she doesn't need to, going out only in a thong, pasties, and pointe shoes. The magenta ostrich feather fans in her hands are the only cover she needs, and she uses them expertly, teasing a peek at her ass when she bends over and flutters the fans like a peacock.

As the song winds to a close, she ends her final pirouette in a simple third position, her fans spread behind her, the rest of her body exposed, vulnerable, covered in glitter and sweat.

The crowd and performers watching from the wings, myself included, erupt into whistles and applause. Ever a prima ballerina, Estelle bows gracefully as dollars and cheers rain onto the stage. Pushing her glasses up, she smirks before prancing offstage.

Felix emerges from nowhere, pushing past me to collect the tips.

My heart is a lump in my throat. Not even a word of encouragement before our finale?

Still, I tap into that confidence from my last number, determined that even if Felix is mad at me, even if I fucked up the chance to be selfish for once in my life—we're here to dance. And we will.

I saunter onto the stage to help pick up tips (the silks I had been planning to fuss with onstage got moved to earlier in the show, due to my lateness). I bring the Easter basket, overflowing with tips, onto the stage with me. As I reach my mark, a chime descends through the theater, the twinkling sound bright. The remixed fiddle plays right as a spotlight illuminates me.

I pose with the basket, leaving my back turned to Felix. Without looking, I can feel his approach. Each step he takes, every breath builds toward the drop into the opening a cappella line of Francesca.

The crowd hushes at the sudden change in mood.

Just as the piano hits, Felix's fingers grasp the red fabric, tugging it gently on my left hip. As if startled, I pretend to gasp, dashing away as the fabric pulls away from me.

Across the stage, I pretend to be mad when the guitar strums, lamenting the missing fabric until I realize how hot my leg looks now, playing it up for the audience with a few bump and grinds that feel too playful for my own emotions. Out of the corner of my eye, Felix caresses the fabric, wrapping it around his neck like a scarf.

We lock eyes just as the first verse echoes through the hushed theater. The remixed beat adds a heavy sensuality to the intense yearning of the song.

All of that pales in comparison to the look Felix is giving me. He was supposed to start off cocky and campy, but his expression is wrecked and earnest.

Is this more improv, a play on the direction our onstage bit took?

It's everything I can do to follow our choreography, instead of running into his arms. But color after color, we dance together, a push and pull. The mood is heavier and the exchanges we improvise are so much more heated than we've ever rehearsed; there is a sensuality on this stage we've never reached before. Is it because of our date last night, or the aching tension between us from this afternoon? Perhaps it's both, and everything else too.

Near the end of the bridge, Felix sinks to his knees once more, crawling toward me with his heart exposed across his vulnerable expression. I give up on pretending I don't want him, and hold out the end of the purple for him. The final piece of my skirt becomes an offering, a silent plea for him to expose all of me too, to leave me merely in my gold thong and bustier.

Felix tugs as he rises to his feet, and I spin as we've rehearsed, wrapping myself back up in the length of purple fabric until he catches me, dipping me easily. In that moment, everything feels right. I am exactly where I need to be.

The crowd cheers, Rudy catcalling, a "woo" from Olive, and Jorge whistling over it all.

Felix is supposed to take off my bustier now, hold it up as one last moment of triumph and then toss it away, because I'm his real treasure. That's what we've rehearsed.

Instead, my hand slides up Felix's chest and around his neck, burying under the red silk draped around it to caress his pulse once more.

Frozen by my touch, he looks down at me, pupils blown dark, eyeliner smudged with sweat. His inaudible moan hums against my palm, throat bobbing between the crux of my thumb when he swallows. If Felix is still upset at how I left, I see no signs. I only find want and need and hope in his blue eyes; the same feelings drive the fluttering in my heart.

"Fuck it." As the song fades to a close, I slide my hand around to the nape of his neck, and pull his face down to mine, meeting his lips with a crash.

Twenty-One

Felix

I'm sure the dull roar in my ears is the applause, but everything besides Luck's lips on mine fades into the background. There are no stage lights shining upon us, no audience watching. There is only Luck's half-lidded eyes smiling at me when I pull them tighter against me. I can't feel the way the whole town is staring at us, can't hear how they're cheering in delight—Luck wrapped around me is the beginning and end of my universe.

It's not until I hear my brother's voice shouting, "Sucks to suck, Alvarez! Pay up!" that I realize Luck and I are fully making out onstage, in front of approximately a third of the population of Sleighbell Springs.

I press one last kiss to Luck's lips (chaste in comparison to how my tongue was just down their throat) as a warning that I'm about to pull away.

The tip of Luck's nose and ears turn bright red as they take in the standing ovation, but their smile is smug when they take my hand. We bow together as more bills rain onto the stage from my

Sleigh Queen castmates in the front row, who are all screaming incoherently. Even Miles Dalton is giddy with smug pride as he whistles, even though we only met two months ago.

"Don't forget you have to pick those up, Felix," May teases as she sashays onstage, tip bucket in hand. "You may have finally got lucky with Luck, but you still have a job to do, bendover boy!"

"I've got another job for you after," Luck murmurs.

I raise my eyebrows, looking over my shoulder as I bend over to sweep up the cash. "Oh? Dirty talk? Onstage?"

"Oh, not like that!" Luck swats my hip. "Well, maybe that, too! But no, we still have to get all of the materials back to my uncle."

"And leave the hole open?" I ask skeptically.

"Now who's talking dirty onstage?" Luck smirks as they collect the scattered pieces of their skirt, draping them over my neck as I pick up the tips still showering the floor.

"Thank you all for coming to the first inaugural Sleighbell Spring Awakening burlesque show!" May announces as a campy, upbeat jazzy tune plays. "Let's give all of our performers a round of applause!"

Everyone, the queens, the Sexy Santas, the aerialists, and pole dancers, all pour out onto stage with wide smiles. The cast dances together to the music in various stages of undress.

I silence Aaron and Avery with a glare before their teasing starts, though Dee Pression and Dixie Normous loudly talk shit, as if Luck and I are not standing right next to them. Estelle, Junie, and the rest of the class all exchange their own teasing grins, and a few suggestive catcalls break out from our castmates when Luck draws me to center stage with them to take our bow. The crowd cheers as we all pose for pictures, before we file backstage and the house lights come back up.

"I'm so proud of everyone!" Luck announces, naturally drawing everyone into a huddle with their voice alone. "This was a sold-out show, and so many of you pushed your comfort zones to new levels tonight, and we should all celebrate our success!" They lean in as they pull their robe around them, and everyone closes in to hear what they're about to say. "But we have a couple more tasks to do. I need us to count up a hundred and fifty bucks from the tips so I can pay Thursday back for the hardware supplies in the hearse, and then I need all of us to help Felix replace the parts that are up on the roof with the parts from the hearse. We borrowed scrap from my uncle to get this place reopened, and he's a greedy manipulative asshole, and we need to return everything before midnight. Can I count on all of you to help us?"

My jaw drops. *That's* what Luck was doing? While I was banking on raising the five hundred in tips to pay their uncle, they were off finding the parts to get it all back before midnight? And they're talking shit about how awful Paul is, *publicly*?

"What?" Estelle asks, wrinkling her nose. "Manual labor? I'll count the money."

"I got you!" Rudy pipes up. When our brothers came backstage, I have no idea. But Rudy is shoving a wad of cash at Estelle to count, so he and Jorge (and Olive) are welcome in my book. "We were taking bets from the audience on whether or not you two would kiss onstage. And you did, so I won!"

"You said you were gonna spend it on video games," Jorge frowns. Olive sits between his feet.

"Come on, I'm not a total ass. That was a joke." Rudy shrugs. "Lighten up, Alvarez! This is a fundraiser, and I just made a solid two hundred from banking on my brother's slutty side."

"Excuse you!" I scoff. "Luck kissed me first!"

"We don't slut shame!" Luck crosses their arms The colorful ostrich feathers of their head piece twitch as they cock their head. "But what do you mean? Felix isn't a slut!" Their eyes widen, and a strange sense of foreboding fills me at their frown. "Is he?"

Rudy gives me a panicked look. "I was just kidding."

"I mean, you're not wrong," May looks at her fingernails. "I've had to clean up more than one mess he's left behind in the upstairs lounge."

Aaron laughs. "Yeah, slut may be a strong word, but Felix doesn't exactly have a virginal reputation around town."

"Can we not?" My cheeks are on fire. The way Luck narrows their eyes isn't helping. I can't tell if I'm supposed to be scared or turned on, but right now, I'm both. "Or at least save this for later? You said something about the hearse?"

"Oh, we are definitely saving this for later!" Luck warns, removing the pins one by one. Their glinty expression makes me more excited than nervous. "For now, you get your tight little ass up to the roof and start taking apart anything that belongs to my shithead uncle. The rest of us will get the replacement parts up to you."

"Replacement parts?" I ask, confused. "It's already eleven. We're running out of time."

"Yeah, but it's raining, and we have help." Pulling their headpiece off, Luck shakes out their hair, beaming. "We're not giving that scummy motherfucker another cent, nor are we going to risk any further damage to this place!" Luck huffs. "So anyone who wants Paul Wilson to get egg on his face before midnight can help us swap out the crap he claims is so important that he's willing to sue us and the Sleighbell Stage for them."

Estelle clenches her fists around the wad of singles in her hand. "Oh, that fucker is getting it! He tried to deny my business plan because the name 'wasn't festive enough.' But it's Umoja Aromas! That's literally one of the principles of Kwanzaa!"

"What?" Junie gasps, grabbing Estelle's arm, as shocked as everyone to hear the classy, reserved Estelle call Paul a cuss word. "He did the same thing to me when I tried to start a community organization for the pagans in town! Who made that asshole the gatekeeper of holiday cheer?"

And just like that, all of the Sexy Santas are fired up and ready to help. Rudy and I head to the roof, where I've kept the Sleighbell Stage's toolbox stashed by the door. We make quick work of pulling up the scrapwood and corrugated metal from the hole.

Nome and Aiden bring up the first sheet of galvanized steel within minutes, and we send a rusty tin one back down with them. The clock is ticking—a mere hour to get all of this back in Paul's shed on the outskirts of town—but between everyone helping, I bring the last materials down the catwalk with fifteen minutes to spare.

Luck sighs in relief when they see Rudy and I descend the metal steps.

"You're okay?" they ask, touching my face, my chest, my arm. They may not be having a panic attack this time, but Luck was still worried about me.

"Little cold." I nod to my bare chest and legs; I only had enough sense to replace my dance shoes with boots, but not enough sense to change anything else. I probably should have worn a coat over my harness and tiny shorts, but it's too late now. I'll change when we don't have Paul's threat hanging over our heads. "You?"

"Of course!" Luck bites their lip, eyes downcast. "Apparently Burl told everyone in town about what happened with Paul earlier, and now everyone's decided to blacklist *him* instead. Lucy Decker even volunteered her husband to audit the estate spending, which seems a bit excessive." They give me a small smile. "But, we'll see how he acts tonight!"

"Do it," I say, with no hesitation. "Auditing the estate isn't excessive at all."

Before Luck can respond, Jorge clears his throat from the hallway leading out to the front. "We gotta go, hermane. Clock's ticking."

Rudy and I shove everything in our arms into the hearse, following Luck to Jorge's Firebird. Thursday waves from the hearse, ready to follow.

"Can't I get shotgun?" Rudy asks.

Olive pants from the front passenger seat, her tail wagging.

"Nope, that's her seat." Jorge smirks. "You all go in the back."

Rudy groans, sliding in beside me when I scoot over to the bitch seat in the middle.

As soon as Jorge pulls off, Luck crosses their arms and turns to me in a huff. "So just how many people have you fucked in Sleighbell Springs?"

The rest of us in the car choke and sputter. Even Olive whines at their question.

"Uhh..." My mind races, trapped between my brother and Luck. "The exact number doesn't really matter—"

Rudy and Jorge groan before I can even finish my sentence.

"Bad answer, dude," Rudy mutters.

"It never meant anything!" I insist. Because the number isn't *that* high (despite my castmates teasing), but there is no right answer to their question. "I was trying to get over you, and everyone said the best way to do it was to get under someone else—"

"*Under*?" Luck sputters. "You bottomed, too?"

"Is that surprising?" I retort, fully aware and unashamed of my own proclivities. "You thought I was into *Jorge* this whole time." Jorge groans in disgust from the front seat. "So why is it a problem that I had a fling here and there, or the occasional encounter with other people instead? It's not like *you* didn't sleep with anyone in the past *twelve* years!" I emphasize just how long it's been since that kiss our senior year.

Luck scoffs. "Yeah, people in *New York*! Not our very small town full of gossips and nosy people!"

"People in New York, like Nisha and Twyla?" I cross my arms in an echo of Luck's. I am pretty sure this is not a serious argument. Luck and I have always communicated best through bickering and teasing, so I am willing to take the chance that this will eventually lead to a meaningful conversation. Or a hotter direction. "Yeah, you told me about that night!"

Luck blows a raspberry. "That was one time!"

"So what, I was supposed to stay a virgin here in Sleighbell Springs, while you were discovering yourself in New York?"

"Yeah, duh!" Luck scoffs.

"Would a virgin have fisted you last night?" I push back, fighting a smirk.

Jorge and Rudy groan so loud that even Olive barks.

"Not cool, man," Jorge gags. "Did not need to hear that!"

"Yeah, TMI!" Rudy leans as far away from me as possible, pressing against the door. "Please talk about this later. Much, much later, when you're alone! And your brothers are not trapped in the car with you!"

"Fine," Luck huffs. "But everything you have ever done with anyone else, I want to do too. And then some! I want to do shit to you that no one has ever done before. I need to be first in something."

"Oh, I'll be happy to oblige." My cheeks burn hot, spreading throughout my body. Somehow I knew this is where this conversation—our first fight?—would end up. "But you were my first kiss, for the record."

Luck purses their lips, trying to keep up their jealous facade. I take the opportunity to press a kiss to their cheek. That is enough to make them soften into a smile.

"We're here!" Jorge says as he pulls into Paul's driveway.

"Thank god!" Rudy mutters, scrambling for the door handle before the car's even parked.

From the front window of the house, a curtain pulls back and falls.

"He's not going to shoot me, is he?" I ask, a pang of anxiety hitting me.

"If he does, Thursday is right behind us," Rudy elbows me, before climbing out of the backseat.

"Not reassuring, dude," I mutter, but I follow Luck out of the car to unload all of the scrap metal and two-by-fours from Thursday's hearse.

Paul opens his front door, frowning as he crosses his arms. Thankfully, no shotgun in sight. "You're cutting it close, Felix. It's five 'til. I thought I was about to call up Christian Decker to serve your asses."

I have half a mind to chuck the sheet of scrap metal at his head, but Luck takes a power stance at the bottom of his porch steps, hands on their hips in an echo of how they posed onstage a mere hour ago. Their silk robe billows in the cool air. "Funny, Titi Lydia always says family handles our own business without getting anyone else involved. I wonder what she would have to say about you suing us."

Paul quickly shuts the door behind him. "Now, Luck…"

"'Now Luck,' nothing!" Luck snaps.

The rest of us carrying materials are frozen, watching the power play between Luck and their uncle. Olive paces behind Jorge's legs, cowering from Paul, until she finally jumps back into the car. Arms full of scrapwood, Thursday looks like he's about to interrupt, but I shake my head.

"The first time you stole from us, Lydia insisted family doesn't sue family, that family business should stay private," Luck seethes. "Every single dollar you drained from the estate, we could have taken you to court for. But we didn't, because family doesn't sue family."

"Too late now, isn't it?" Paul sneers. "You got your inheritance."

"But Luis and Efrain aren't old enough to get theirs yet," Luck smiles. "So Titi Lydia is still on the hook for another few years. And strange, how quiet she's been about how much is left in the estate for them." They pause, adding casually, "You know who all was at our show tonight, Uncle Paul? Burl was there, as were many of your peers from the Chamber of Holiday Cheer. And you know how people talk in Sleighbell Springs." They tsk, almost theatrical in their blatant emotional manipulation. "And wouldn't you know, the Deckers were there too! Lucy made a point to let me know her husband would be happy to audit the estate spending, just for my peace of mind."

There's a long moment of tense silence, before Paul huffs, waving a hand at Jorge. "What are you waiting for, put that shit away!"

"Remember, dear Uncle Paul," Luck spins in their duck boots on the Wilsons' front walk. They sashay towards the car, calling over their shoulder, "Family doesn't sue family. That protects *you* more than it protects *us*. You'd be better off if you remembered that. Especially now that you've shown your true colors to the whole town. Titi Lydia can't blame me for airing out family business, when it's you who's been showing your ass."

With a cocky smirk on my face as Paul glares at me, I heft the rusty, bent scrap metal I'm carrying higher onto my shoulder, and walk past him into his backyard. The clock is ticking, and after we show Paul exactly what he's worth (nothing more than discarded scrap), Luck and I are overdue for a conversation. After all, I don't want their mind to be on anything else but me, when I give them the marks I owe them.

Twenty-Two

Luck

"All right, kids." After dropping Rudy off, my brother parks his Firebird in the driveway of our house, instead of opening the garage. "It is midnight-fifteen. Olive and I are going to go hang out at the shop and get some work done." Jorge turns to the backseat, grimacing as he looks at us. Olive looks back at us too, her tongue lolling out of her mouth. "When I come back home, in say, a couple of hours, I'd like if we could all be on PG behavior."

Guilt pangs my chest. "You don't have to leave—"

"Oh, no! I do." With a dry laugh, Jorge turns back to the front. "Happy you two finally got your shit together, but I also live in the basement. Just remember I am right below you at all times, and I do not need to hear my best friend and my sibling getting busy." He fakes a gag. "But I understand this is new, and you both had a stressful day, and you got some shit to work out. This is for the best, if I just go fuck around with some cars for a while and leave you to do whatever it is you need to do."

"Can you make it three hours?" Felix asks. "Three and a half, maybe?"

I smack his arm. "He doesn't need to leave at all!"

"How about this?" Jorge huffs. "Olive and I will just sleep at the shop tonight! Enjoy it while you can, because this is the only time I'm doing this. You're welcome. See you in the morning. Get out of my car."

Felix nods for me to open the passenger door; he's still in the middle seat, glued to my side as if he can't stand the idea of any space between us. Not that I want him to scoot over! No, Felix is exactly where I want him to be.

Jorge is peeling out of the driveway as soon as he makes sure we can get in the front door, and Felix is kissing me as soon as it's closed behind us.

Any guilt I had about my brother feeling like he wasn't welcome in his own home vanishes when Felix cups the back of my head, his kiss slow and unhurried and perfect.

"Are you okay?" he asks against my lips, pulling away just enough to look at me.

I nod, chasing his kiss.

But Felix steps back, eyebrow raised. "Are you okay?" he asks more firmly.

"Yes!" I huff.

He levels a look at me. "Because you were so upset earlier that you stole my truck and drove it God knows where and didn't text or call or—"

"I'm sorry," I murmur, chagrined.

"Don't be sorry," Felix huffs. "*I'm* sorry for causing you so much stress in the first place. I was just...worried sick about you. I still am. Do you want to talk about it?"

My throat catches. Normally, after a day like today, full of anger and panic, exhilaration and pride, I'd sit in the Eldorado to feel closer to Dad. Or comfort myself with hot cocoa con queso like

Mom used to make. But right now, I only want Felix with me. I want to find comfort in the future, not the past.

"Can we talk in the shower?" I ask. "I'm really cold, and sweaty, and I have rust all over my hands from carrying that sheet metal."

Felix nods for me to lead the way, and I bring him to my en suite bathroom, where Felix installed a walk-in shower and clawfoot tub for me when he renovated it years ago. It was my attempt to make my parents' bedroom less theirs and more mine, so Luis and Efrain could have their own rooms when they started high school, and Jorge could keep the basement to himself. The walkout patio door was the only way he could get in the house without assistance when he first got home from the hospital, and the quiet and privacy is good for his mental health. My parents are still all over the house, but their old bedroom feels more like mine.

Turning the heat lamps on, I drop the thin silk robe that I never bothered changing out of because we had to drive like mad to Paul's house. The gold thong and bustier follow, as do the pasties I peel off moments later.

While I pull the pins out of my hair (I never even had the chance to style it properly earlier, but the rainwater and head pieces did most of the work), Felix turns the water on and peels off his equally skimpy clothes. The spray fills the shower stall with steam, but I only have eyes for Felix—his broad shoulders, the crease of his bare hip, the pale smooth skin of his muscular thighs.

"I imagined us in here together," I admit when he guides me under the delightfully hot spray. "When you installed it for me, and were showing me the taps. I imagined turning on the water then, when we were fully clothed, just so we'd have an excuse to be in there naked."

Felix's cheeks pinken as he lathers up a wash cloth. "If I'd known you were thinking it too, I would have." He takes my hand, pressing a kiss to my knuckles before scrubbing my palm, my wrist, my arm with the soapy cloth. Erasing all of the rust and the sweat and the aches, Felix warms any of the cold left in my bones after the long, heavy day.

Was it only this morning that I woke up in his bed, deliriously happy and aching from the inside out?

Leaning against the tile wall, I sigh, tilting my head back as Felix pampers me, washing me gently and kissing my body as he goes. Felix is on his knees in front of me, when I finally feel brave enough to speak. He's treating my gnarly feet as reverently as the rest of me, gentle between the toes shaped by a youth spent in pointe shoes.

"Your truck is at the graveyard," I murmur.

Felix looks up at me, his wet curls dark auburn and plastered to his head. He waits patiently.

"I think I needed to let go?" I sigh. "I was angry at them, at myself, at Titi Lydia and Paul. And I've never really let myself be as angry as I needed. Because it was an accident—not my fault for inviting them to my show, or their fault that it happened to be snowing. It's not their fault they trusted Lydia to put us before her husband." A bitter smile graces my face as the hot water rolls over the crown of my head, running down my body.

Felix's calloused hands massage my foot in his lap.

"I never let myself be angry about the unfairness of it all, never truly let myself grieve for myself, because I was always putting my brothers first. And when I thought I might lose the car my dad never finished restoring for me, I just..." I huff, unable to explain. Already, I feel so exposed, just remembering my time at the graveyard.

"I'm sorry, again," Felix frowns. "I should never have put your car on the line. I should have insisted that Paul use something else as collateral, or borrowed the money from May or someone." He huffs. "I was just tired of begging for scraps, or trying to wheedle my way into more credit with the hardware store. I was desperate, because how else could I get the theater reopened in time for your show?"

"Stop apologizing about the car, cariño." I cup his cheek, smirking at how flustered Felix gets whenever I call him that. His already rosy blush deepens. "I already said I understood, because I would have done the same thing. Trust me, I get it."

Despite the flush of his cheeks, Felix wrinkles his nose in annoyance. "You shouldn't though. You give way too much of yourself for everyone, at your own expense. You should be more selfish."

"Fine," I say primly, dragging my foot up his thigh. "You want me to be selfish? You have a lot more to be sorry for than making a scammy deal with my uncle."

When I press my foot directly between his legs, Felix blanches. He looks up at me, blinking the water from his eyes, but he doesn't pull away. On the contrary, he shifts so his dick is pressing against the ball of the foot he just washed. "For what?"

"For fucking other people! In public!" I huff in mock annoyance, though a part of me is genuinely crushed that it wasn't *me* he was fooling around with in the Sleigh Queen lounge. "Or whatever else you might have gotten up to, with God only knows who!"

Felix rises up on his heels, pressing his engorged dick against the top of my foot instead. I can't tell if he's wet, or if it's the shower, but his front hole is hot and slippery when I flex my toes. "Oh, is *that* what this is about?" he murmurs, leaning forward to sink his teeth into my thigh.

The yelp he pulls out of me is more in surprise than pain. Like him, I don't pull away in the least, offering my thigh for him to feast on.

Felix soothes the mark with the flat of his tongue first, then his lips. "You're upset because you were martyring yourself for your brother, when he was never in the running at all?" He looks up at me, kissing his way across my hips and belly. "Are you mad that you and I could have been together this whole time, and instead I was entertaining other people?"

I purse my lips, a little annoyed he's read through me that easily. "Maybe."

"Luck, we are right on time for each other." Felix leaves another bite mark on my opposite thigh. I keep my yelp inside this time, instead moaning at the exquisite pain of the bruise he leaves. He kisses the red imprint of his teeth gently, strong hands gripping my hips. "I meant what I said earlier. I'll happily, eagerly, do everything either of us have ever done and more, and I'll enjoy it far more than I have with anyone else. Because they're not you, Luck. I've never loved any of *them*."

Like a chord struck in a quiet room, the word hangs in the air. The earnestness in his blue eyes makes my breath catch in my throat. "Felix, I-"

Jaw tight, Felix shakes his head. "Don't say it."

Annoyance flares through me. "But I was gonna say it back."

"Nope!" Felix presses a chaste kiss to my mound, before he spins me around by my hips. I gasp in surprise, balancing myself against the tile wall. Scalding hot water pours down my back and over my ass. His lips drag kisses down my spine as he murmurs, "We're going to take this slow, the way we both deserve. And that means no big declarations on the second day of our relationship, in the middle of an emotionally and sexually charged conversation."

"Fine," I snip. Deep down, I'm touched that Felix isn't rushing into this. We haven't had a real chance to talk seriously about what we want from this relationship yet, other than each other. "But I do, you know. Love you."

Felix snorts, sinking his teeth into the meat of my ass cheek. "I know." I arch my back to give him more to bite. His hands caress my skin, spreading me apart with his thumbs. "I owe you some marks, but first?"

I cry out when his hot tongue drags up my clit, delves into my cunt, and slips back down to suck me greedily. The tile wall and his firm grip on my hips are the only reason I don't collapse in a trembling mess on the shower floor. Felix always looks good, but nothing beats the sight of this man on his knees for me. Red curls plastered back, eyelashes thick with water that frame his blue eyes, and his face buried between my ass cheeks. Even after only one night, he already knows me so well; I'm coming all over his face in minutes.

"Felix?" I ask, fighting for breath as I come down.

He hums to prompt me to keep talking, tongue swirling around my clit. Normally, coming back to back would feel overstimulating, and it does! I am overwhelmed by him. But I need more of it, more of him. I'm already so close again.

"Which hole, front or back?" I manage to ask.

"Hmm?" he asks, brows knitting together.

"What hole should I take, when I fuck you after this?" I reach back, raking my nails across his scalp to bury my fingers in his hair.

His eyes roll back and the deft, steady circles of his tongue falter. The sudden swipe of his tongue in the opposite direction has me crying out again, trembling as another orgasm overcomes me.

"Tell me, cariño," I croon once I've regained the capacity to speak, thrilled at how eager he is to bend over for me. "I want you on your knees, begging for me to fuck you, a greedy little slut for my strap. So, what hole do you like better? Front or back?"

"I've..." Felix bites my ass cheek again, as if trying to reclaim some semblance of control. But I just pull him tighter against me, keeping his mouth there until I can't take the pain anymore. "Front," he pants once I let him up. "I've never actually had anyone fuck my ass before."

A beam of delight bursts in my chest. "Perfect. I'll claim your front hole for myself tonight, fuck you so good you forget anyone else ever had you there." I smile over my shoulder. "Then tomorrow, we'll start training that back hole. And no one but me gets to use it."

Felix groans, kissing the red welt his teeth left. "If you want, some other time," his blue eyes blink through the spray of water as he stares at my own asshole, still exposed for him under his hands, spreading me open. "I would love to return the favor." With a smirk, Felix spits on my hole, dragging his tongue along the tight muscle.

My delighted laugh comes out more like a moan. Bracing myself against the tile wall, I press my ass back against his hot mouth. As tempting as it would be to let him fuck me right now, I have other plans. I indulge him a few moments more, letting him worship me until I'm on the verge of collapsing, before I push him away.

"Clean yourself up, cariño," I murmur, pulling Felix to his feet with a gentle grip on his chin. I kiss his cheek, his jaw, his ear. "It's my turn."

Felix's eyes widen. He scrubs himself off in record time, before I've even got out of the shower. Bundling me up in a towel, Felix hurries me along to the bedroom. I can't help but laugh at his unabashed eagerness.

"Felix, stop rushing me," I murmur, pushing him back onto the mattress. "I want you to get on all fours, close your eyes, and wait like a good boy, okay?"

"Fuck," he moans, scrambling to kneel on the bed. I catch him looking a couple times, his expression feverish in anticipation, as I adjust the straps of my harness, select a dildo I think Felix will like and coat it with lube. I bought all this stuff from Jingle My Bells years ago, determined to move on with someone new. But they've gone unused, other than on myself, imagining a moment like this with Felix. Always Felix.

Though in all of my fantasies, I'd never imagined Felix would moan quite so sinfully when I fucked him, would arch his back quite so deep when I pressed a hand to his lower back. His muscles ripple and flex as he moves with me, his hole dripping sticky down our thighs when he takes all of my strap. His eyes are wide, cheeks flushed red when he looks back at me, babbling my name and praise and demands for more, harder, faster. Is this how he felt last night, when he fucked me with his fist? Elated and honored and so incredibly blessed to witness him coming apart and begging for more?

For as long as we've known each other, I've always thought Felix was a kind person—a secret sweetheart who was so cute when he was annoyed. But now that I've finally pulled him close, now that I'm pulling him apart and into me, my Felix is full of surprises. Generous, adoring, freaky surprises.

Luckily for Felix, I fully intend to make him forget anyone else has ever crossed his mind, however long that might take. I will give him everything he's begging for and then some. Even after he's satisfied and spent, I'll still take care of him, fuss over him as much as he does me, to make sure he knows how much I cherish him. One hour, one night, the rest of our lives. Felix is mine, and selfishly, I want to keep him.

Epilogue

Luck

"Are we ready?" I call, fiddling with the keys in the entryway. My mom's wreath on the front door has a robin family nesting in it, and the babies squawk impatiently for their parents to feed them lunch. I shove my feet into my espadrilles, relieved it's finally warm enough to go without thick socks and heavy boots. "Hello? Anyone here?"

"We're already in the garage!" Jorge yells back. "We're waiting for your slow ass!"

"Yeah, hurry up, we're gonna be late!" Luis calls, the stickler for time in our family, as always.

I huff in annoyance as I open the door to the garage, which is already open wide to bright blue summer skies. Bertha and Leann hang prettily on their racks, but I am not biking anywhere today.

True to my brother's word, all three of my brothers—copies of each other in their baseball jerseys, hats crammed on their brown curls—are crammed in the backseat of the Eldorado with Olive wiggling all over them. Her tail waps poor Efrain in the face.

Alone in the front passenger seat, Felix greets me with a smile. "You ready?"

I nod as I settle into the driver's seat, wordlessly greeting Dancer with a touch to the rabbit's foot and St. Christopher charms, dangling from the rearview mirror. I've been practicing this part for weeks, just getting in and sitting on this side and thinking about driving it one day. "Nine years is long enough. Time to see if we actually got this baby working."

"Maybe we should be testing this when we're not running late for our game," Luis mutters.

Jorge smacks him. "I checked everything myself this morning. She's running fine. It's Luck we gotta worry about."

"Thanks," I deadpan.

"I believe in you, Luck." Ever the sweetheart, Efrain, my favorite brother (at the moment) squeezes my shoulder from the backseat. "And since Jorge is the umpire, it's not like they're gonna start without us."

"Thank you, Efrain," I smile at him from the rearview mirror.

"Kiss ass," Luis teases.

"Keep it down back there, boys!" Felix teases, laughing along with my brothers when Jorge smacks the back of his head. He's just as much part of our family as he has been my whole life, only now? Now he's my partner, my lover, my future, in addition to being my best friend. Someone my brothers can count on as much as they do me.

Jorge, Felix, and I have spent countless hours over the past few months getting the Eldorado into working shape. Obscure parts have been ordered and salvaged. Weekends have been spent researching where this bolt came from and what happens if we just don't put it back. I've relearned all of the lessons my father taught us when we were kids. Jorge and I have shared them with Luis and Efrain, while they're home for the summer.

Titi Lydia, while she hasn't gone so far as to leave her husband, has been coming over more on the weekends, especially since Luis and Efrain are back. She's teaching them all the recipes my mother once taught Jorge and I. After she leaves, we tell them what Mom did differently, because Mom's cooking was always better than Titi's.

Uncle Paul stays home, probably trying to figure out how to get his spot back on the Chamber of Holiday Cheer after he was voted out by the board. I'm sure he'll weasel his way into some influence again—he always does—but he wasn't around when Felix's business approval was voted on at least.

Krampus Construction is up, running, and in high demand. Probably because Felix is still a pushover, even now as a contractor. Still, he pays himself a living wage, instead of relying solely on tips from Sleigh Queen to get by. I'm wearing one of the T-shirts Aiden Cane designed for him, complete with an illustration of an incredibly ripped and shirtless Krampus in a tool belt and hard hat over his horns. Perfect for my sweet and sexy Scrooge.

Felix smiles back at me from the passenger seat, and I realize I'm staring at him (as always), instead of focusing. I am on a mission to take yet another symbolic step in my journey of reclaiming my life: driving my brothers to their baseball game. Just like Dad used to do when we were young. Though instead of T-ball or a high school varsity game, we're going to a game for the beer league Dove Devlin sets up every year. Jorge is an umpire, and Luis and Efrain are outfielders for their team.

With surprising ease, I turn the key in the ignition. The engine roars to life, purring over the radio that buzzes with static, before settling into the station my dad used to listen to. Instead of classic rock music, the station now plays early 2000's hits. All five of us burst into song, hollering along with Green Day. Olive woos along with us from Jorge's lap.

Putting the top down, I let Dancer run for a bit before putting her in first gear, waiting for the anxiety to hit.

But it never does. Instead, I simply find myself excited to finally take my Dancer on the road and show her off to everyone, to spend time with my family. Easing off the clutch, I roll out of the garage and into the street.

With the sun on my face, the wind in my curls, and Felix's thigh under my hand between shifting gears, I drive towards the outskirts of town. The candy-cane mailboxes, snowflake-adorned light poles, and cheesy lawn ornaments that decorate Sleighbell Springs year-round accompany us. Biking has always made me feel free, but alone. Driving with my partner, my brothers, my family—this is something else I've been holding myself back from. Something else to regret.

But what is the point of healing, of reclaiming my power over grief and loss, if I don't have regrets? I'm driving with my family now, connecting with the life my parents wanted for me, not the one they left me with, and loving Felix each and every day; that's what matters.

No matter how unlucky my life has been, or what else the universe has in store for me, I am doing what I can to make sure that everything will work out for the best. From now on, I will be taking my chances. For my own sake.

SET LIST

First Half

Life's a Drag - Intro Song	May and Felix
Titi Me Pregunto - Bad Bunny	Sexy Santas
Toxic - Britney Spears	Dee Pression
Dontcha - Pussycat Dolls	Junie Hendicks
Ray of Light - Madonna	Clair in the air
Call Me By Your Name - Lil Nas X	Aaron/Nome
Feeling Good - Nina Simone	Ginger Snap
Pink Pony Club - Chappel Roan	Estelle Du Nord
Francesca - Hozier	Luck/Felix

Second Half

WAP - Cardi B	Sexy Santas
Pour Some Sugar On Me - Def Leppard	Dove Devlin
Pony - Ginuwine	Junie Hendricks
Larger Than Life - Backstreet Boys	Trans Mascs
Her - Megan Thee Stallion	Dixie Normous
Rapper's Delight - Sugarhill Gang	Estelle Du Nord
Earned It - The Weeknd	Ginger Snap
You Don't Own Me - Lesley Gore	Luck Alvarez
I Am What I Am - La Cage Aux Folles	May North

Want more of Sleighbell Springs?

2026 Releases
Drag me Home Again – J.E. Joyce – January
Better Lait Than Never – Ellie Blackbourne – February
For Luck's Sake – Cozy DuBois – March
Trimmed with Love – J.J. Hart – April
Brew Me Wrong – LS Phoenix – May
All Booked Up – E.J. Stoll – June
Tattooed Tidings – Lila Grey – July
Worth Melting For – Bellamy West – August
Sugar, Spice, and Cozy Nights – Ilsa Rayne – September
Thursday the Thirteenth – Anthony Scott – October
Silver Bells Stalker – Evie Noir – November
Happy (Endings) for the Holidays – An Epilogue Anthology – December
Check out the series page on Amazon! More releases coming in 2027!

Acknowledgements

First and foremost, a huge thank you to J.E. Joyce for your stroke of genius with dreaming this series up, putting in the work to herd all of us into formation, and bringing the series to fruition! Shout out to all of the other Sleighbell Springs authors for making this shared universe such a fun place to be! I love all of our shenanigans, and I can't wait to read all of your fabulous books!

Full credit for the cover design goes to Marge Turingan (@caravelle_creates) for the fabulous cover design for this book, and all of the books in the series! They are all so beautiful, and you did amazing work bringing Luck and Felix to life!

As always, I have endless gratitude to Mikko Lahna of Quick Fox Editing. We have one brain cell between the two of us, and it only wants to read trans/queer idiots to lovers. Felix and Luck are the way that they are purely for our entertainment!

To my beta and sensitivity readers (you know who you are!), thank you for your candid and supportive feedback in being the first readers to experience this story and helping me shape Luck, Felix, their friends, and families into the lovely people they are. Special kudos to one sensitivity reader who inspired me to put a hit out on Paul in the series Discord. Don't worry, readers, he's getting what's coming to him!

So much credit goes to the local drag and burlesque scene in Minneapolis for being fabulous and providing so much inspiration for this book! I am so privileged to live in a place where we have so many wonderful artists and performers, so many venues who host shows, and so many people to tip the artists generously! Support your local drag and burlesque performers!

Finally, I also want to recognize of my neighbors here in Minneapolis, and all of Minnesota. Pretty much the entire time I've been working on this book, our state has been occupied by ICE, and thousands of my neighbors have been detained without due process. Two Minneapolis residents, Renee Good and Alex Pretti, have been killed by ICE agents. The whole state has banded together to protect our community through rapid response teams, food drives, legal support, and mutual aid efforts.

With every book and series, I donate 25% of profits to a beneficiary organization. For this book, current events has made the choice simple for me, and I've selected the Immigrant Law Center of Minnesota, which provides free legal assistance to low-income immigrant and refugee families. If you'd like to learn more or donate as well, their website is: www.ilcm.org/. I encourage everyone to get connected with your own community organizations, and if you can, please donate (money, time, and/or energy) to mutual aid efforts in Minnesota and other impacted communities. To quote the late Paul Wellstone , "We all do better when we all do better." Community, whether it's in person, online, or in the bookish sphere, is how we move forward, together.

ALSO BY COZY

If you enjoyed this book (or if you didn't!), please kindly show your support by leaving a review and telling your friends about it. Honest reviews and word-of-mouth recommendations make it possible for indie authors to keep writing. Thank you!
Want to read more by Cozy?
Check out their books at cozydubois.com

***Confession* Series**
Book 1: *Loving Lee*
Book 2: *Love on the Sunny Side*
Book 3: *Tempting Tara*
Book 4: *Carte Blanche*
Epilogue: *Finally Phineas* coming 2026!

Summer Weddings in Solberg – Rereleasing Spring 2026!
Petty Roots
Familiar Faces

Standalones
Glimmer in the Dark

Short Stories
"Dad, Are You..." — part of *Bi All Accounts: Volume 1.*

About the Author

Cozy DuBois (they/them) thought writing fiction was a long-lost hobby. A longtime lover of romance novels, Cozy has renewed their love for writing by telling stories for and about LGBTQ+ people. They hope to bring more books into the world that represent the complex and entangled relationships between friends, lovers, and chosen family found in the queer community they love.

Based in Minneapolis, they enjoy life with their partner, two hound dogs, a regal queen of a cat, dozens of houseplants, and a garden that has seen better days. Find them with a beverage in hand on a patio anytime the temp is above freezing or planning their next vacation when it's not.

Connect with Cozy on social media or via email updates at cozydubois.com for announcements about upcoming releases.

www.ingramcontent.com/pod-product-compliance
Lightning Source LLC
LaVergne TN
LVHW040142080526
838202LV00042B/2995